Guardian of the Red Butterfly

A Novel
by
D. S. Cuellar

壱

弐

Guardian of the Red Butterfly
Extended Edition

Visit us on Facebook at
Guardian of the Red Butterfly

Cover Design by Roslyn McFarland

Special Thanks to:

Editors:
TJ Monarch
Dana Cuellar
Paula Sherwood
Pauline Suite

Technical Support:
Ryan Wintersteen
Kevin Dye

And a special thanks to David Morrell for his encouragement and correspondence.

四

Chapter 1

Tied spread-eagled to the hotel bed, not moving, he lay unconscious from a sedative and was gagged with his own necktie. Dressed only in boxer shorts, Senator Dalton's mid-forties body was a testament to the long, hard hours he put in at the gym.

Karina barely noticed his well-defined muscles as she pulled a tranquilizer dart from the senator's neck and placed it on top of his day planner on the nightstand. It was 2:35 pm and, according to the Senator's schedule, he was supposed to be resting before his speech to the International Human Trafficking Subcommittee. Karina folded Dalton's clothing and placed them on a chair, making sure the blazer was on top. The U.S. flag pin on the blazer lapel gave the beautiful, dark-haired woman an uneasy feeling.

Up until now, Karina hadn't noticed the elegant features of the two-room suite. The walls were a light camel brown with off-white trim. Sheer curtains matched the trim; heavy drapes were a rich tapestry of browns, gold, and burgundy. After surveying the room, Karina's troubled eyes came to rest on the tall, solidly built man sitting in the corner easy chair.

"Hurry up, Karina. You're wasting time," Victor said, waving the tranquilizer gun in her general direction.

His stone-grey eyes clearly projected the severity of his demands.

After removing her soft-soled shoes, Karina unzipped her pale blue housekeeper's dress and let it slide down off her slender figure to the floor. Standing at the end of the king-size bed, her hands shook ever so slightly as she untied the Senator's legs. Never before had Victor made this type of demand of her. His usual tactics included insults, bullying and an occasional twist of the arm. The intense jealousy Victor routinely displayed caused Karina to believe he would never allow another man to touch her or her touch another man. This out-of-character command brought on a fear that erased all hope of her ever having a normal life with Victor. She had no idea exactly how far he was willing to use her in this blackmail scheme.

Karina's eyes filled with tears as she watched Victor set down the tranquilizer gun on the table and walk up directly behind her.

"Now the underwear," Victor demanded. Karina reached for the senator's boxers.

Victor grabbed Karina by her hair and pulled the young Russian beauty's delicate and attractive body back into his. With a vulgar condescending whisper in her ear, he said, "Not his. Yours."

"You're a bastard," Karina mumbled in broken English. She didn't have the strength to resist Victor's intimidation as he guided her hands down to her hips. With her hands trembling, she slowly slid her panties down.

Victor's smile was wide and wicked as he said, "So what does that say about you? It says, my dear wife, that you will do what I say when I say it, or that pretty little face of yours will be no more."

Karina gave Victor a defiant look which was rewarded by a hard back-handed slap across her face. The blood on her quickly swelling lips was bitter. She carefully wiped it away with her fingertips.

"Don't you dare bleed on the senator," Victor snapped. "The photos are supposed to show passion, not pain."

Victor had Karina remove the gag before untying Dalton's hands. He then picked up the camera and ran off a few frames to make sure the camera was ready. "Now, darling, do what you do best and make it look real. Let's see some sweat."

Karina straddled the body of the high-ranking senator. She massaged his bulge over his soft cotton boxers until she felt him become fully erect. She then kissed his mouth and chest. She caressed her own body in mock ecstasy for the camera. Every cell in her body screamed in protest. The sweat on her body was produced not from the sensual act she was performing, but from the rage she felt toward the man she married. Despite the wide range of intense emotions she was feeling and the distraction of the camera flash, Karina still felt the stirring of the arousal stemming from between Dalton's thighs.

Without warning, Dalton's hands reached up and grabbed Karina. One hand landed on her thigh, the other grabbed at the front of her bra, pulling it away and exposing one of her breasts. Before she could scream, Victor put his hand over her mouth and whispered in his wife's ear, "Keep going. His groping only makes the photos look more realistic." Karina could hear the motor on the camera winding away, one damaging photo after another.

It didn't take much effort to pin Dalton's arms to his side. There was no resistance from him, only the slightest movement of his head.

With every click from his camera, Victor's gratification fattened. After a couple minutes, he said, "That's enough." He gave the senator a sarcastic look before punching him hard enough to knock him out. Addressing his wife, he said, "I wouldn't want you to enjoy it too much."

The statement stunned Karina. The only intimacy she had ever displayed was for Victor. His current comments and actions, though, seemed to indicate that she was just one of the many other girls with no name that he had sold off to the highest bidder. Karina's new deep contempt for Victor, and for herself, manifested itself in words she unwisely blurted out.

"Anything for my dear husband. You mean like this?" Karina removed her bra and fondled her own breasts. She began rocking and grinding over the Senator with a passion not previously displayed. Small pleasing moans escaped from her tender supple lips.

Victor grabbed Karina by the throat and pulled her off the bed with such force it nearly crushed her windpipe. He slammed her up against the wall so hard she felt the drywall crack immediately upon impact. The physical pain of Victor's torment was keeping up with the mental pain he was unleashing on her.

Both were doubling in their intensity in a manner he had never revealed to her before. Victor held her against the wall, staring angrily into Karina's tear-filled blue eyes. Her legs and feet dangled like a puppet as her toes barely reached the floor.

"You ever disrespect me in that manner again, I will kill you." The fury in Victor's face seemed to fill the entire room. When it was evident his wife was about to pass out, he loosened his grip.

In a low shaky voice Karina said, "Why did you make me do this?"

"I want to own Dalton. These photos are a transfer of power. What was his is now mine. Like this mouth of yours."

Victor kissed Karina viciously, then a second time more gently to remove the small amount of blood still on her bruised lips. Fighting for air, she tried to push Victor away. The gesture only enraged him and he tightened his grip on her throat again. The ticking from his Rolex magnified in Karina's ears, her other senses also heightened due to the extra adrenaline pumping through her veins. She was keenly aware of Victor's intense cologne he used to mask his body odor and cigarette smoke permeating from his clothes.

Within seconds, her consciousness began to fade. Karina tried to focus on the ceiling fan, but its circulating blades only pulled her mind into a downward spiral, promoting the illusion of drawing her deeper into this hell on earth.

"It is this mouth of yours that I love so much that will one day be your demise. Fortunately for you, my dear, that isn't today. I still need that mouth for other things," Victor hissed. A second later he released Karina. She collapsed to the floor, gasping for air.

"Now clean up this room and get rid of any evidence of us being here. I'll pick you up when your shift is over." Victor grabbed the Dalton file and took one last look around the room. "Don't forget your underwear, Karina. I happen to like that color on you."

Victor stood in the doorway of the adjoining rooms. He took a step back into the room to remove the flag pin from the senator's lapel and placed it in his pocket as a souvenir. At that moment Karina noticed the bed in the other room was not empty. Dalton's aide, an attractive, thirty-something blonde was tied to the bed in the same manner as the senator.

Disgust nearly made Karina throw up as she saw the woman's dress hiked up mid-thigh. The aide's panties were torn away and hanging loose down around one knee.

Before he closed the door to his room, Victor glanced at the woman in his bed and then at Karina. "She turned out to be more useful than just a way in."

In that moment, Karina realized she lost everything she never really had.

"What I do, Karina, is none of your business." The chill in Victor's voice was close to an explosive stage. "Now what is it you want?"

"Nothing, Victor," the betrayed wife said as she shut her door.

In the bathroom, Karina stood naked before the mirror, clutching a towel in front of herself, a shame so deep no amount of soap and water was going to make it disappear. She tried to wash away the red welts on her neck, all it did was sting. Mascara streaked her face, her lipstick all but gone around her swollen lips.

Walking to the edge of the bed, Karina dropped the towel and climbed back onto Dalton. This time every grind of her hips, every touch to his body were for other reasons. Ones she couldn't explain to anyone, especially herself.

Karina threw her head back, her long, black hair cascading down her back, her pain nothing but a bittersweet ending to the situation she was now in. Sweat ran down Karina's face, the vein in her neck pounded in an increasing rhythm with her heartbeat, and the sound of her heavy breathing filled the room.

In her mind, she could picture the images that Victor had taken of her with Dalton and as she played them over and over in her mind, her anger grew. Soon the images were scrolling faster and faster. As the flash of the camera caught up to speed, it was like watching one of those old-time movies as the flicker rate danced in her head until she could no longer fight the pain that had consumed her with rage. She felt the energy building within herself start to surge throughout her body and without remorse gave into the moment at hand letting her consciousness fall away. She could feel herself slowly floating down as her head come to rest on his chest. All she could hear was the rhythm of her heart and exhaustive panting as her sweat soaked body involuntarily shivered uncontrollably.

Chapter 2

The room was quiet. The cursor on the computer screen blinked, waiting for its next command.

The arrow slid across a series of files that the appeared on the monitor and stopped over one marked, Karina. With a click of the mouse, the file opened and revealed two more files. One was for documents and the other for images. With another click, the image folder was opened and there, covering the screen, was a picture of a beautiful twenty-year-old Karina.
A small female hand reached up and touched the monitor and caressed the picture.

"Mama?" a young female voice gasped.

With another click, the documents folder was opened. The oldest file was close to twenty-five years old. She clicked and there was a short pause before the document was opened. Karina's biography at the time showed she was twenty years old and originally from Russia. Scrolling down a few words stood out. A company, Masato Enterprises. A name, Romanov. A price, $50,000.

The name Romanov was highlighted. The command to open was made and a family tree appeared and showed a lineage that went all the way back to Peter the Great.

After she clicked out, the curser launched the image file once more. Opening one image after another Karina's story was chronicled, going from being a frightened twenty-year-old to a year later being married, then onto what appeared to be five years later, a woman in charge of the family business.

Then there was a fifteen-year-old picture of Karina, eight months pregnant. Again, the gentle hand passed over the monitor and stopped over the extended belly. The young hand left the screen and was brought up to the young girl's lips. She turned and saw herself in a mirror.

Oksana was a young, beautiful, innocent girl, all of fourteen, who lived such a lavish but sheltered life. All she ever wanted was to have some friends her own age to play with. Oksana could hear footsteps on the wooden floor coming down the hall as they approached the office.

The door to the den opened and her father, Victor, entered along with a business associate. The room was quite luxurious and there were a few pine logs burning in a one of a kind fireplace.

"Can I pour you a drink, Marcus?"

"Sure, a Scotch would be fine."

"Scotch it is."

Marcus looked around the den and saw relics and trophies from all around the world.

"I see you are a collector."

"Yes. I like only the best. Take this fireplace, the stones were once part of a castle off the coast of Scotland. When I was there last, I saw what was the remnants of a fallen wall that had once guarded the castle. I had enough of the stones shipped over to do the job."

"Yes, it's very beautiful."

Marcus looked at a photo of Karina and Oksana. "How is your family?"

"You mean, how is Karina?"

"You have owed me ever since you decided to keep her for yourself."

"I had bigger plans for her."

"And now?"

"The plans have changed and they are already in motion."

As the two men looked around the room, neither of them could see that Oksana had hidden under Victor's desk before they entered. Victor did notice his laptop was missing but didn't question its disappearance in front of his client.

Under the desk, Oksana was trying not to move as she listened in on the business conversation going on just across the room. Oksana saw a file labeled: Clients. She opened the file and found a list of about 50 men. She skimmed down the list and found a name beginning with Marcus. Marcus Bennett.

She clicked on his name and found he had made eight purchases ranging from $15,000 to $20,000.

Marcus was looking at a small shelf that contained a dozen small items. He picked up the lapel pin of an American flag, "So you think Dalton is the best? I hear you are having some difficulties with him."

"That pin you are holding was his. In fact, it is still in working order so make sure you don't close the clasp. Besides the pin, I took his dignity. He'll come around. If he doesn't, he knows what will happen by not cooperating when we ask him to."

The men took a seat on the couch and Marcus set the flag pin on the coffee table in front of them.

"How are things working out with Morrell in Portland?"

"He's proven to be a very nice asset. He knows firsthand what will happen the next time he falters. We broke him years ago."

Oksana opened the file marked, Morrell. More pictures, and this time of a highly decorated police officer, his wife, and their two sons. As the pictures unfolded, the images of the boys showed them progressively getting older and they seemed to be following in their father's footsteps becoming police officers themselves.

One was a seasoned detective and the other was holding his shield, having just made detective himself. What was missing was, there were no more pictures of the wife. The boys' mother seemed to be missing from the family dynamics.

"What about the older boy?"

"I'm not sure if he's gone rogue or not but we will know soon enough."

"How's that?"

"If his father doesn't come through for us, he just might lose his younger brother to a tragic accident. You have to be mighty careful these days in such an unpredictable town. You never know for sure who you can trust."

"Speaking of trust, are you sure you can trust this guy, Masato?"

"We have a deal in place that will ensure us a high volume of product for the best price with very low risk. So far it has been working out nicely."

"What do you have on him?"

"Every man has a price. Once you know the one thing he can't live without, you have the man."

"The item you were able to acquire happens to be a missing heirloom of the Masato clan and it is already on its way to be reunited with them as we speak."

The door opened to the den. Karina entered and excused herself. Victor was irritated by the interruption. "What is it?"

"It's getting late and I was just looking for Oksana."

"Obviously the girl is not here so you can close the door and leave us to our business."

Karina looked at Victor with a hard stare then she looked at the foreign businessman with disgust as she turned and closed the door.

"Where were we? Ah, yes, our partnership with Japan and the great northwest."

"How is Masato working out?"

"He's done very well ever since the merger. His family's export business gives us the perfect opportunity to use all of our assets as one and in the last five years, sales have never been better."

As the men continued to talk business, Oksana opened the Masato file. Inside the file, she saw another file labeled, Aiko. She clicked on it. Among the contents were a few pictures of a geisha holding a sword wearing a brightly colored kimono. Below the picture, it read, Samurai Geisha. It was hard to tell her age behind the white-faced makeup. Oksana was curious so she googled the word geisha.

The translation of geisha into English would be "artist," "performing artist," or "artisan."

Oksana's eyes skimmed down the page quickly.

Geisha often began training at a very young age, sometimes as early as at 3 or 5 years and stages of geisha training lasted years.

Oksana scrolled further down.

"Coerced sex" and "virginity". Nowadays, a geisha's sex life is her private affair.

Oksana felt she had read too much and closed the search. Then she heard that phrase again.

"The girl."

"Speaking of, you said I would be getting one of the best you had to offer, and I have yet to see my prize."

"Patience, my friend. I know you are eager to claim such a gift."

"That sword I acquired for you is worth double the asking price on the open market. I gave it to you as we agreed upon for such a special gift. I take it that also means she is still a virgin and a virgin is what I am expecting to get."

Oksana went back into the file labeled, Marcus. Something she had missed before, one line under transactions was open and had a statement, katana valued at of $40,000. Next to the price was a JPEG file. Oksana opened it and could not believe her eyes. The shock caused her body to twinge involuntarily and her knee kicked the inside of the desk wall with a loud thump.

Both men stopped talking and Marcus gave a concerned look to Victor. Victor set down his drink and walked over to behind the desk and saw

Oksana sitting on the floor clutching the laptop.

Victor grabbed her by the arm and pulled her up. Oksana could feel his powerful, intense grip squeeze her tight. She was frightened that if he jerked any harder he might break her arm.

Victor took the open laptop from her and set it on the desk where it came from. He saw on the computer screen what she was looking at that had scared her so much. Next to the amount of $40,000 was a picture of Oksana. Victor hit a button and the word "save" momentarily appeared over Oksana's picture, then the screen went dark.

"It looks like you no longer have to wait, Marcus. Your gift has been here all along."

Oksana was shocked by the words coming from the man who had raised her as his own.

"What's the matter, Oksana, did you really think I was your father? I've known for years and now you and your mother are going to pay the ultimate price for such a betrayal." Victor looked at Marcus then back at Oksana. "Actually, he's the one paying the price."

Oksana jerked her hand free and started to run for the door, but Victor grabbed her by the hair and stopped her in her tracks. He spun her around and as he did, he backhanded her hard enough to make her nose start to bleed. The pain and dizziness she felt was nothing compared to the fear that was running through her body.

Marcus stepped in trying to help protect the girl, as well as his investment. "Careful now, Victor, I did pay double."

Victor handed Oksana over to Marcus. "Sold."

Chapter 3

Marcus led Oksana to the plush couch and let her sit down. He sat down next to her as Victor headed toward the door. Before Victor could reach the entryway, Marcus had already turned off the table lamp. As Victor exited, he hit the light switches at the door. He took a look back and saw only the light of the fireplace lighting up Oksana's cold, blank, distant stare.

As Victor closed the door he could see life leaving her eyes and when the door closed, Oksana could feel the oxygen leave the room.

Marcus removed his jacket and laid it over the back of the couch. "I will be the one to take care of you now."

He noticed Oksana was looking at the flag pin. He picked it up and handed it to her. "Here, this is yours as much as anyone's." He then removed the gun from his shoulder harness and set it on the nightstand. Oksana looked at it but did not flinch.

Marcus' voice was without sympathy, "If you think you can take it, take it."

*****

When Karina could not find Oksana, she went to the upstairs office that was once the bedroom next to theirs. She had been using the computer to pull up the interior security cameras to find her daughter. She saw what had happened in the den. The nightmare scenario had come true. Victor had found out Oksana was not his, and now she knew she had very little time to save her daughter.

She looked around the desk for anything she could use. On the corner of the desk was a picture of Victor. In the picture, he was standing in front of a fifteen-hundred-pound blue marlin he had caught off Cape Cod from his latest fishing trip to the states.

Karina took the picture frame apart and broke the glass on the side of the desk, leaving an eight-inch shard of glass in her hand. In doing so, she winced as it cut the palm of her hand. She looked down and saw a trickle of blood. She grabbed a piece of tissue from her pocket and stemmed the bleeding. She quickly hid the shard of glass.

As Karina exited the upstairs office, she was surprised to see Victor at the door.
She was acting a bit nervous. Victor took a quick look around the office then took Karina by the hand and led her to the master bedroom. He wasn't about to let her out of his sight. Victor could feel the sweat forming in Karina's hand.

"What's wrong?"

"It's getting late, I need to find Oksana."

"She's all right. I just said goodnight to her."

Victor was executing his plan of selling off Oksana and getting the wife he considered to be a traitor, out of the way. He had found out years before, during a routine medical exam, that Oksana could not have been his child. Their blood types did not make that possible. Since then, this plan was put into motion, and today was the day to execute.

Just like Victor could read men, Karina could read Victor and knew his pattern of desire. She knew she would only have a small window of time, and that time was now.

Karina let Victor lead her to the bed. She sat him down and took a step back to give him a better look and started to slowly undress. As Victor started to feel he was in control again, he let his guard down and felt he would have one more opportunity to screw his wife in retaliation for the years he felt she took him for a fool.

There was no doubt, she was beautiful and she knew how to please him. He watched as she reached back with both hands to undo her bra. What he didn't see was, that was where she had hidden the shard of glass. She slowly slipped the piece of glass out from under where her bra clasp clipped together.

Victor stood up in front of her, took her left

hand and placed it on the forming bulge in his trousers.

As he went to raise his left hand to touch the side of her face, he saw some blood in the palm of his hand from when he had taken her hand as they left the office.

Before he could react, Karina stabbed Victor under his left arm and into his side. Instant hot pain ran through Victor's side and weakened his legs. "You bitch!"

Karina took advantage of the moment and kneed Victor firmly in the groin. Pain on top of pain dropped Victor to his knees. Karina stepped back toward the door and just before she walked through, Victor's words stopped her in her tracks. "Your daughter is no longer the daughter you once had."

*****

Karina was trying to make her way downstairs but her legs felt weak and she was unsure of each step she took. By the time she reached the bottom and saw the door to the den was closed. Adrenaline took over and she found her footing. Once at the door, Karina saw a flicker of light that came from under the bottom of the door.

Her mind raced but she had to be careful, so she turned off the hall lights, put her hand on the doorknob and slowly turned. She made a small gap in the door, opening it just enough to see inside.

She saw that Marcus had his back to the door. That's when her attention went to Oksana. All she could see was one of her legs sticking out from under his body. In her mind, she was dying with every second that passed. That's when she saw the gun sitting on the stand at the end of the couch.

Upstairs, Victor had made his way to his feet, slumped onto the side of the bed and pulled out his cell phone. He made a call and growled a single command, "Send me, Bogdanoff."

As Karina cautiously slipped inside the door, all she could hear was her own heart beating out of her chest. She knew she had to calm herself, she took a deep breath as she moved across the floor in her bare feet. She focused on the sound of the crackle that came from the fireplace, not the sounds the couch was making as Marcus was shifting his weight over Oksana.

Marcus opened his eyes after releasing himself and saw Oksana looking over his shoulder in a blank stare. Then he noticed something caught her gaze. The dancing light from the amber flames had created a mirror effect in Oksana's eyes and Marcus caught a glimpse of a figure standing behind him. He turned and saw Karina holding his own gun on him.

"Get off of her," Karina's voice trembled.

Marcus slid out from between Oksana's legs and covered himself.

"Now take your coat and cover her."

As Marcus turned to grab his coat off the back of the couch. Karina caught a glimpse of some bloodstains on the couch and on the inside of Marcus' thigh. Karina did not remember even pulling the trigger but Marcus was surely dead.

From outside the house, the guard at the front gate was so focused on the soccer match he was watching on his iPhone and listening to with his earbuds, that he didn't notice the flash through the thin veil of curtains that hung in the den.

Karina took Oksana by the hand and helped her off the couch. As she stepped away, she kicked Marcus' trousers that were on the floor and heard a set of keys jingle. She took the keys and grabbed her daughter and ran out the door.

Once out the front door, Karina initiated the key fob and saw they went to a 2015 Ford Explorer. She put Oksana in the back seat and got her strapped in. Karina scrambled to get in behind the steering wheel, looked in the mirror and saw her baby with that still blank, thousand-mile away stare. Oksana barely moved, but her hand did slide off her lap, and when she opened her hand, she was still holding onto the flag pin. Karina knew she had to keep herself together but it was hard to see past the tears that had overtaken her.

Karina took a deep breath and tried to compose herself as best she could.

In the distance, the guard at the gate felt his phone vibrate and saw the incoming phone call that interrupted his game.

Karina saw the guard turn around and start walking in her direction. He had his phone on speaker as he was talking to Victor. Next to Karina in the front passenger seat was a man's hat, presumably Marcus'. Karina put it on and pulled down the front brim leaving just enough room to see out from under. She started the Explorer and headed toward the gate.

The guard saw the Explorer coming his way and a silhouette of a man behind the wheel. He raised his hand to slow the vehicle and inquire who it was, but by then it was too late. Karina hit the gas and clipped the guard as she drove by, knocking the phone out of his hand and him to the ground. As the phone flew through the air, its final transmission before it struck the ground and smashed apart was Victor's voice asking, "Do you copy? I said, 'do not let anyone leave the premises.'"

Karina removed the hat and tossed it in the seat next to her, gripped the wheel firmly, and crashed the gate.

Chapter 4

Broken rays of sunlight passed through the dingy curtain causing little flickers of light to dance around Karina's face, highlighting the toll fifteen years had taken on her. She was sitting on one of two beds in a grossly stripped hotel room. The chipped paint from the walls was the least of the damage. Some wall cracks ran so deep and with holes so wide, you could see into the next room. No room seemed to be without a draft and signs of rodents that sleep by day and forage by night. The windows were so warped and weathered by the elements, time refused to let them open. The drapes were so tattered their original color could barely be detected.

Terror had once again assaulted Karina's mind and emotions. Her fingers twisted and weaved with each other like she was trying to complete a puzzle. A lifetime of fear had been unkind to the 40-year-old-woman and her once long, luxurious hair had since been cut to shoulder length.

Karina stood up to watch the figure in the bed next to hers. Satisfied the child's breathing was normal, she walked quietly to the room adjoining hers.

From the doorway, she watched Portland Police Detective Steven Morrell rummage through a small duffel bag.

Karina walked back to the bed and kissed her daughter on the forehead, then joined Steven in the next room, closing the door behind her. She sat on the edge of his bed and was trying to figure out exactly what Steve's motives were for returning to the now dilapidated hotel. Karina asked, "Why did we have to come back here?"

"I need to validate your claim as part of the relocation process."

"I can't believe these are even the same rooms. I do recognize the wallpaper though, what's left of it anyway."

"Are you sure this is the same suite where Victor took the photographs of you and the Senator?"

"Yes. Victor paid someone to get me on the payroll as a maid for a couple of weeks just prior the conference. This was my floor, and this was definitely the room. I am sure of it."

Steven ran the timeline through his head. "Not long after the conference, there was a fire that gutted half of the hotel. Then the economy tanked. Since this hotel is over 100 years old, there was no way it was feasible to restore it back to its original luster.

In the meantime, it's been ransacked over the years for its fixtures and copper pipes, hence the holes in the walls."

"Steven."

"Yeah."

"I'm afraid."

"There's nothing more to be afraid of. You're going to be safe from now on."

Karina placed her face in her hands. Her comments were muffled and difficult for the detective to hear. "You can't know that for sure, Steven. No one can."

Steven barely glanced at her during his response. "I imagine you have a lot on your mind."

"I made a mistake fifteen years ago."

"I don't think you consider your daughter a mistake," Steven studied Karina's reaction to his comment.

"Oksana isn't a mistake, but what I did to get her was." Karina's troubled blue eyes filled with tears.

Steven tried to console her. "And getting away from Victor was definitely not a mistake."

The air was heavy, like a cold fog that hung in the room. Steven walked over to Karina and placed his hand on her shoulder. "It won't be much longer and the two of you will be in a safe location."

Karina sighed as she glanced toward the room she just came from. "I hope she's dreaming about the things that most young girls do, like going to the mall with her friends, playing dress up, or getting a puppy. She should not have to worry about waking up every day, fearing for her life."

"When did Victor realize she wasn't his daughter?"

"I think he's known for a while. He's been patiently waiting for Oksana to come of age so he can get top dollar for her." Karina shuddered as she thought of all the times Victor seemed to examine Oksana like a menu item.

"What happened? Why now?"

"I'm here because of Oksana. She doesn't deserve this. No one should have to experience what happened to me."

Karina ran her fingertips across her jawline. Her memories could still bring back the pain she went through by Victor's hand.

Steven saw the pain in her eyes and the courage it must have taken to risk their escape. "You've done a great job with Oksana. She looks like a brave little girl who's been through a lot."

"You don't know what we've been through and don't act like you do."

"Then tell me. The more you tell me the more I can help you." Steven wanted to tell her how beautiful she was, but he knew that was what Victor was taking advantage of, the way men looked at her as a prize.

"Steven, do you have any children?"

"No."

"If you did, would you kill to protect them?" Karina knew the answer before she asked the question. "Of course, you would. Every day I thought about running but I knew I would be risking our lives."

"You're a very brave woman and a loving mother."

"Brave? I may have just killed my daughter."

"I'm not going to let that happen. We have resources in place that will give you and your daughter a fresh start. I've already got the process started for witness relocation. When this is done, all you will have to worry about is where you want to live."

"You don't understand. Victor has a worldwide network that doesn't play by your rules. He'll be coming."

Steven could see he was maybe asking too much, but he wanted to know what was worth risking both their lives over. "Karina…"

Karina's emotions erupted. "Victor Pankov is a monster! Not only did he use me for his blackmail schemes but he is also in the business of human trafficking and he used me as his whore."

Karina saw the look that came over Steven's face that couldn't be hidden. A look of shame that he could only imagine, but knew she had to carry with her.

"Are you telling me he was going to sell his own daughter?"

Steven could see the fear that controlled her world come over Karina.

"She's not his daughter." The words didn't feel any better admitting them out loud.

"Why did you wait so long to leave? You could have left when she was younger, avoiding the stress on both of you."

"I guess I wanted to believe Victor thought Oksana was his."

"Then who is her father?"

"Victor likes to find dirt on officials he can use to blackmail them with. If he can't, he'll find a way to put that person in a compromising position. He will do whatever it takes to get the job done, including using his own wife. This particular time, I got pregnant."

"Oksana."

"Yes. He must have figured it out and now that she is of age, he's made a deal to sell her."

"Sell her? To who?"

"The highest bidder."

Steven could feel his insides churning. Knowing what he knows from the stories his father has told him about the world of human trafficking, he asked, "Are you saying he already has a buyer?"

"Had. I killed him. After we got away, I paid a man off with my wedding ring to bring us across the border. Once across, he still wanted more so I did what I had to do for my daughter's safety."

Steven asked, "Do you know anything about the man or his business? Maybe what he did for a living?"

"He brought a crate with him. Something Victor needed to further another part of a transaction. For what, I do not know. I did hear a name. It sounded Japanese. Sapporo."

"There is a Sapporo, Japan. It's on the northern end of the island. They held the 72 Winter Olympics there."

Steven saw the toll all this was taking on Karina. With each breath, her body was beginning to wilt like a flower right in front of him. He slid closer to her and put an arm around her. He let her rest her head on his shoulder, trying to give her some comfort in knowing she was going to be safe now. As much as he wanted to keep holding her, he knew she also needed her space and room to breathe. After hearing her story, he thought she was one of the most courageous women he had ever met.

*****

A couple of blocks away from the Vintage Hotel was a five-story parking structure. On the rooftop, a SWAT officer laid dead, a bullet hole directly between his eyes. His deceased partner had been dragged and dumped next to him by their assailant, Karl Bogdanoff.

Bogdanoff was former Soviet military and performed his job with a vengeance. When the

Soviet Union was dissolved in December 1991, the Soviet military was left in a state of uncertainty. After a few years, Russian forces began to withdraw from parts of Europe. After that, reforms announced reducing the armed forces to a strength of one million, thus reducing the number of officers of which, Bogdanoff had held the rank of Commander. He had given his entire life to them after his wife and child were killed in an explosion by terrorists. He had decided to go after the men who had taken away his family and fight fire with fire. To do so he would have to play by terrorist rules. Once he found out which faction had done this to his family, he was determined to give them the same pain he felt, and he went after their families in return. He started by kidnapping a relative of one of the men responsible. He decided he wasn't going to kill them, but he was going make them wish instead that he had. He began by sending home body parts of the people he kidnapped. He got a taste for it and eventually began working for whoever had a cause and the right amount of money to justify him venting his anger. For now, that man was Victor Pankov.

Once Bogdanoff was sure there were no other threats, he crouched down behind the edge of the rooftop. He focused his rifle scope on two SWAT officers approaching on foot across the roof of the Vintage Hotel. Off to the right, two more SWAT officers prepared to repel down the side of the building to the window above the room where Steven and Karina were holed up.

Emptying the life out of people was second nature to Bogdanoff. He visualized his victims as objects of his favorite past time, target shooting. A sociopath since his early teens, the killer lacked any emotion that might interfere with his profession. Only once in his 30-year career as an assassin did he make a mistake. That misjudgment resulted in the scar across his right cheek.

For half of Bogdanoff's career, he was an obscure and one-man operation. In the last few years, he had been successful in training and perfecting his new team of skilled assassins. Today, those trainees would demonstrate Bogdanoff's skills as a hired gun instructor. He watched with anticipation, the scene that was about to unfold. The two SWAT officers, Taylor and Bergin, were standing side by side preparing their ropes for descent. Their legs were aligned for a single shot from Bogdanoff.

The assassin had positioned himself between two cars with the sun at his back. He raised his rifle into position and peered through the scope at the approaching SWAT officers. This was no routine assignment and everyone had their designated location. As the other two SWAT officers unfamiliar to them approached, Officer Taylor took notice.

Through his scope, Bogdanoff put his sight on Officer Taylor's head. He slowly panned the crosshairs down and aimed at his thigh. Bergin stood next to him and Bogdanoff knew that with only the slightest effort, he would be able to cripple both men with one shot. He aimed, took a breath, exhaled and with the next beat of his heart, was ready to squeeze the trigger.

Just as the two SWAT officers approached Taylor and Bergin, Taylor said, "What's up guys, I have the building's schematics—"

Before Taylor could finish his sentence, the searing pain of a bullet passed through his thigh, instantly relieving him of his ability to stand. As he fell, he saw Bergin fall in a heap next to him. In his last moment of clarity, Taylor saw the two approaching SWAT officers withdraw their pistols with silencers at the ready.

Chapter 5

Steven and Karina sat across from each other on the hotel room beds fine-tuning the details of her and Oksana's escape and relocation plans. Gazing into Karina's eyes, Steven saw fear and determination for the safety of her daughter. Her stress-lined face showed signs of betrayal left by the forceful hand of Victor. Beneath those lines, Steven detected beauty, strength and courage. Karina noticed the look on Steven's face went from concern to panic in a manner of seconds.

"What is it, Steven?"

Steven was staring at a red dot from a laser sight on the wall behind Karina's head. The dot of the laser snapped quickly onto the center of Karina's forehead. Without thinking, Steven pushed her to the floor, pinning her between him and the bed, his body acting as a shield to protect her. Karina held Steven so tightly he felt her heart beating against him. Adrenaline raced through their bodies and the heat of the moment sparked emotions inappropriate for the situation. In the midst of the chaos, the soft scent of Karina's skin wrapped itself around Steven and he found himself very much caring for this targeted woman.

"He found us! Victor found us!" Karina said. "I've got to get Oksana. Let me up, Steven!"

"Don't move."

Steven rolled off Karina, pulled his Beretta out from his side holster and handed it to her.

"Do you know how to use one of these?"

Karina took the gun safety off and racked back the slide.

Steven grinned. "Apparently you do."

In one swift movement, the detective reached up with one hand and pulled his duffel bag to the floor next to them. Taking out a bulletproof vest, he instructed Karina to put it on. Steven then pulled out a second Beretta and went through the same actions as Karina did with hers.

Sweat and worry became more pronounced on Karina's face as she watched the handsome, sandy-haired detective flip open a cell phone and start punching numbers. "How can we trust the person you're calling? You promised Victor wouldn't find us."

"I'm rerouting the number through the operator."

"If this call doesn't work, we'll all be dead for sure."

Steven wanted to offer her reassurance, but he could not find any words of comfort to guarantee their outcome. He dialed 911.

"Nine-one-one operator. How may I help you?"

"I'm a detective with the Portland P.D. Badge number nineteen fifty-nine. I need you to connect me to Captain Frank Morrell."

Steven observed a startled reaction in Karina's body language at the mention of the name.

Karina spoke in a hushed voice, "Frank Morrell was one of the names I saw in my husband's files. Victor only kept a file on you for one of two reasons; either Frank is a sworn enemy or he is corruptible."

"Hello, this is Captain Morrell."

In a hesitant voice Steven said, "Hey Dad, I think I need your help."

*****

Captain Frank Morrell walked out onto the rooftop. A SWAT officer handed him a bulletproof vest to put on.

"Hold just a minute, son."

Morrell handed his phone to the SWAT officer while he put the vest on.

When the phone was back in his hand he said, "I'm on the scene with a high priority situation. Whatever you've got going on will have to wait." Morrell moved the phone away from his mouth to shout at fellow officers, "No one fires unless I say so. I don't want this to blow up in our faces if it turns out to be some bogus signal."

Steven could hear men shouting back to his father; he couldn't make out what they were saying except for one word, Vintage.

"Dad, —"

"Steven, I'll call you later." Captain Morrell disconnected the call. He switched to a walkie-talkie, demanding that everyone look sharp and hold for his command.

*****

The look on Karina's face was one of confusion and fear. "You don't understand. They're not here to help rescue us. He wants Oksana." She quickly crawled away from Steven and toward the room where her daughter lay sleeping.

Steven decided to take a chance and call his father back directly.

"This is Captain Morrell."

"Dad, don't hang up. I think I'm your target."

"What are you talking about? Where are you?"

Chapter 6

As quietly and carefully as she could, Karina opened the two inner doors that separated the two hotel suites. She sighed with relief seeing that Oksana still asleep. Crawling over to her fourteen-year-old daughter's bed, Karina laid her head on the pillow near her.

"America was supposed to be a place of freedom and dreams," Karina thought to herself. "It has offered me nothing but the same lies and bondage as Russia. Oksana and I will always be someone's prisoners."

Tears slid down her tired face and landed on the long strands of her daughter's dark brown hair. Karina carefully woke Oksana and instructed her to lay on the floor. Next, she pulled down the top mattress and stood it up between them and the window as a barrier. She instructed Oksana not to move and told her that she would be right back. Karina then made her way across the floor into the other room. She closed one of the inner doors as another barrier protection for her daughter and went to sit next to Steven.

"What do we do now, Detective?" Karina asked.

*****

Steven tried to use a cracked mirror on the wall to see outside while still talking on the phone with his father.

"I'm on the second floor, west side of the Vintage Hotel. Where are you?"

"I'm on the roof of the building just south of you, off your southwest corner," answered Captain Morrell.

"Well, call off your guys directly across from us to the west. I see laser sights probing our location."

Captain Morrell scanned the upper levels of the parking garage to the west, then panned to the right along the west side of the hotel and up to the roof with a pair of binoculars. He lowered the binoculars and checked the laptop an officer held for him. On the display was a grid of the area with a red blip in the center of the picture.

"Steven, we've got a top priority signal coming from your location."

"I just got here a couple of hours ago Dad, and I haven't called anything in."

"I've got SWAT in teams of two all around you."

Steven crawled over to the west wall below the window. He put his cell phone on speaker and raised it to the bottom of the window, using the face of his phone as a mirror to look across to the other buildings. As he held up the cell phone, the laser sight from the sniper's rifle bounced upward projecting a dot on the ceiling. Steven tilted his cell phone trying to refract the laser sight back to its source.

Bogdanoff realized his location was jeopardized. He quickly disassembled his rifle, hid it in a toolbox labeled Northwest Heating and Air, and left his perch.

Since the cell phone was no longer close to Steven's mouth, he spoke louder so his father could hear him, "What are you planning?"

Captain Morrell replied, "My men are moving in on the location of the signal now."

"Stop," Steven interrupted. "The area is not secure."

Before Captain Morrell could call off his men, Steven heard the front door to the adjoining suite burst open as the SWAT team used a hand-held battering ram to gain entrance, followed by Oksana's scream for help.

Karina sprang up and went for the door handle of the adjoining room.

Sounds of breaking glass, gunfire and screaming emanated from Oksana's room.

"Oksana!" Karina yelled out in desperation.

Steven grabbed Karina and pulled her back down just as a barrage of bullets ripped through the inner door.

As Captain Morrell tried to get a better look from his location, he told Steven, "My men should be securing your location—"

"I think your men are down and there's a sniper in the upper level of the parking structure across the way."

Yelling at the officer standing next to him, Captain Morrell said, "Get me a new line of sight from that parking structure into the hotel."

The officer grabbed his gear and rifle and headed off to scout the new location.

Returning to his conversation with Steven, Morrell said, "Steven, are you alright?"

"I'm here. I think Pankov's men might have taken out your SWAT team. They knew you were coming, and when."

Oksana's screams sent absolute terror throughout the rooms. Karina tried to crawl toward the door to her daughter's room, but Steven held her back. "We don't know who's on the other side."

"I don't care, Oksana needs me!"

The sound of heavy footsteps approaching their door from the hallway caused Steven and Karina to freeze. They watched the door handle turn slowly. When it finally opened, a SWAT officer stood in the doorway. Bleeding profusely from multiple gunshot wounds, he fell forward into the room, dead before he hit the floor. Steven hurriedly pulled him into the room and closed the door. He confiscated the officer's gun and a couple magazines of ammunition.

"Karina, stay low and away from the windows," Steven instructed.

It seemed like an insurmountable amount of time had passed when their door opened again and a second SWAT officer stood in the frame. He flashed them a reassuring smile and for a moment, they allowed themselves a breath of relief. It was then that the officer pulled from his left side, Oksana. He placed her in front of himself, his hand on her shoulder.

Karina gasped and pointed her gun at the officer. Steven reached out and put his hand over her gun, lowering it to the ground.

As Karina said, "Oksana, come here," Steven crossed the room to take Oksana from the officer.

When he was close enough, the officer let the girl go to her mother. Steven turned to walk with Oksana and the SWAT officer pistol-whipped him to the ground.

For a second time, Karina took aim at the SWAT officer.

*****

From the sniper's previous position, a SWAT officer looked through his rifle scope across to Steven's room. He saw a woman pointing a gun at a fellow officer. On the radio he said, "Captain, I have an armed suspect. I have a clear shot."

Morrell replied, "Take it."

*****

Inside the room, Karina's gun was aimed at the officer's head. The assassin, posing as a SWAT officer, had his gun pointed at Steven.

Disoriented and bleeding, Steven crawled across the floor and grabbed Karina by the pant leg, urging her to get down. She ignored him, staying focused on the assassin instead. With her free hand, Karina pushed Oksana to the floor alongside the bed.

A split second later, Karina was shot from behind, through the side of her neck. She dropped to her knees and grabbed her throat.

The gun she was holding fell to the floor next to Steven.

"Mama!" Oksana screamed in Russian.

The assassin moved in quickly and grabbed the girl. He placed his hand over her mouth to muffle her screams and backed his way out of the room, using Oksana as a shield. Steven could do nothing except take Karina in his arms.

"Hold on Karina, stay with me."

With a callous sneer on his lips, the assassin said, "I don't think she's going to make it, and neither are you. Mr. Pankov sends his very best and that would be me."

As the assassin made Steven his new target, Oksana bit him on the hand he was using to hold her. Her action caused him to jerk and curse, momentarily taking his eyes off Steven. That distraction gave Steven the opportunity to pull Karina across his body to use her as a shield and grab the pistol lying next to him.

In the assassin's attempt to get a better grip on Oksana, his hand reached across her chest covering the US flag pin. He aimed at Karina and fired. The bullet hit center mass of the bulletproof vest she was wearing.

Almost simultaneously, Steven raised his gun and fired a shot, hitting the assassin under the chin and killing him instantly. As his body fell backward his grip on the flag pin broke the clasp and the pin fell to the floor.

"Oksana, come to me," Steven insisted.

Scared, heartbroken and confused, Oksana wasn't sure whom to trust. The man she depended on to keep them safe had failed. Now her mother was dying. Picking up her flag pin, Oksana turned and ran down the hall. She didn't get far before another man, also dressed in a SWAT uniform, stepped out from the second bedroom and blocked her escape. Steven continued to call her name, but it was too late, the man in front of her was not about to let her go.

Karina, dying in Steven's arms, attempted to speak, but blood slurred her words. "I need to tell you something."

"Shhhh. Lay still, help is on the way." Steven's hand was on the side of Karina's neck trying to stop the bleeding.

In a barely audible voice, Karina said, "Fifteen years ago, when the photographs were taken—"

Steven yelled out the window, "Officer down! We need medical!"

"There was one man I did sleep with that my husband didn't know about."

"Save your strength, Karina. You don't need to confess anything to me." Tears in Steven's eyes made it difficult for him to focus on her face.

"Steven, you need to know..."

Steven could sense Karina's desperation. "Hang on, Karina, save your breath."

Karina arched her body as the pain pulsated through her. "Steven..."

Steven gripped her hand but could feel that Karina was not gripping him back. He could feel the life unwillingly leaving her body. "Stay with me." Steven turned and yelled out the open window, "Where's that medic!"

The shouting gave Karina a surge of energy, enough to tell Steven the truth about her daughter. "Promise me, Steven. Promise me you will take care of Oksana."

"With my life, I promise."

"She is Dalton's daughter." The words were barely out of Karina's mouth when she took her last breath.

Noise from the hallway made Steven point his gun toward the door.

From the hallway, he heard his father yell, "Steven!"

"In here."

Captain Morrell entered the room with his gun drawn. Steven sat up against the wall with Karina's dead body in his arms.

"It's clear, Dad."

Captain Morrell checked the second bedroom before he informed his men in the hallway that it was all clear and safe to enter the rooms.

"Your signal turned out to be a trap. They knew you would come for the girl," Steven said, his voice defeated.

"What girl?"

Chapter 7

At one of the corners of the Vintage Hotel, an ambulance was parked. The back doors were open and EMT Barry Perez argued with Steven over the injury to his head.

"I've known your father a long time, Steven. You're a lot like him."

Steven tossed an ice pack back to Barry and headed off in the direction of his father. "I used to think so too."

Twenty yards away, Captain Morrell was having a conversation with a SWAT officer. When the Captain violently threw his hand-held radio to the ground, Steven knew the news he'd just received wasn't good. Out of the corner of his eye, the Captain saw Steven approaching. He barked an order to the SWAT officer then walked toward his son.

"There's no sign of the girl and the two officers who were covering the back of the hotel are dead," Captain Morrell said. "They've been stripped of their uniforms."

"And that makes it at least, what, seven?" Steven asked.

"This is your case, son. Who do you think Pankov sent to take out Karina?"

"More than likely, a guy named Bogdanoff. Karina told me about him being Pankov's ace," Steven looked at his father. "How did you know we were here?"

"I didn't know you were here. I received orders to hit this location hard and fast. It was a priority call."

"You've got six dead SWAT officers, a lost 14-year old girl, and your call got Karina killed."

"You don't know what you're talking about," retorted Captain Morrell.

Steven and his dad were only a short distance from a group of uniformed officers. The raised voices of father and son created a lull in their conversation. The eyes of the entire group concentrated on the interaction between them.

"Don't you men have a job to do?" Captain Morrell snapped.

The officers disbursed, leaving the exchange between the two men to continue.

"What are your men doing to find the girl?"

"We lost the signal, Steven. I've got men searching the area along with any security cameras that may have recorded something pertaining to this investigation."

"And now Pankov's men have her."

"Why would Pankov go through all this to kidnap his own daughter?"

"Oksana is not Pankov's daughter, Dad. She's Dalton's."

Captain Morrell examined his son's face for any trace of untruth. "You'd better have something more than just the word of a dead hooker."

"Karina was not a prostitute. She was Pankov's wife."

"It still didn't keep her from spreading her legs for her husband's associates." Disgust spread over Captain Morrell's face.

"And how would you know that, Dad?"

"Never mind how I know. You still don't have any proof that the girl is Dalton's daughter."

"If Oksana was Pankov's daughter, then why would she have a homing signal that you were instructed to respond to? It would make no sense for you and a SWAT team to launch a full-scale rescue for a prostitute's daughter."

The Captain stared coldly at his son, his impending comment interrupted by the ring of Steven's cell phone.

"Steven Morrell." There was a slight pause before he said, "Okay."

Within a few seconds, a dirty, dark brown, unmarked police car drove up and parked a short distance from Steven and his dad.

"Who's that?" Captain Morrell asked.

"You'll see."

Steven walked to the vehicle and entered the front passenger side. He gawked at the man behind the steering wheel. The man's rancid body odor was nearly unbearable, his clothes only a little more than rags. A gold detective shield hung from his neck.

"I know it's been awhile, but I haven't changed that much," said a voice coming from the back seat of the car.

Steven's head whipped around to stare at his brother Kyle. His older sibling wore a Bluetooth in his ear and had a laptop computer on his lap. The dark, sandy blond, blue-eyed brother also sported a wide grin on his face.

"What the hell, Kyle? Is this your new partner?"

"Not quite. I didn't want to blow my cover, so I had Jackson here help me out. I just picked him up on his third strike. We made a deal. He keeps his mouth shut and helps me retain my cover and I let him walk. Isn't that right, Mr. Jackson?"

Jackson smiled and nodded his head.

"So, you got a felon driving a company issued car. Nice touch, Kyle. I hope you know what you're doing."

"Always, little brother. Always." Kyle looked through the windshield and caught sight of his dad. "I see the old man is here. Did you tell him you called me?"

"No."

"Does he know it's me in this vehicle?"

"I imagine he does by now," said Steven.

"That must have twisted his shorts when he figured out you called me."

Their comments made Jackson snicker.

"What are you laughing at, asshole?" Kyle snapped. "Get out of here."

Jackson started to exit the car when Kyle tapped him on the shoulder with his handgun. The scared junkie took the gold shield off from around his neck and handed it to Kyle. There was a second tap on Jackson's shoulder with the gun as the detective said, "Now you can go, Jackson. And remember our agreement."

After Jackson left the vehicle, the older brother leaned over the front seat and asked Steven, "So, what's going on? You weren't very specific on the phone about the situation you're in."

"Damn Kyle, couldn't you have found a felon that smelled a little less like a garbage truck on a hot day? Wait, that wasn't Jackson. It's you!"

"You better get used to it if you want to be a real detective and work the streets. I'm just trying to maintain my cover."

"As what? A 10-year-old jockstrap?"

"How'd you guess?"

"Let's get out of this car." Steven quickly exited the vehicle. Noticing his brother was still in the back seat, he walked around the car to his door. Kyle knocked on the window with his gun, indicating he wanted Steven to let him out. Steven smiled as he hesitated before opening the car door.

Captain Morrell noticed the arrival of his oldest son but was unable to approach his two boys because of an intense phone conversation with Chief Sorenson.

Kyle and Steven used the opportunity to finish their discussion.

"I need your help, Kyle, to find a missing girl."

"Who?"

"She's the daughter of the woman killed under my watch."

The tone of Kyle's voice immediately switched to one of a somber and professional manner. "I caught part of the situation on the radio, bad news, man. I'm sorry. So, who's this girl?"

"Karina Pankov's 14-year-old daughter."

Kyle whistled. "Your first assignment in and your primary catches a bullet. Coincidence? I was surprised when I heard you had caught this case."

"I was ready and Dad needed me."

"And now how do you feel?"

Steven didn't answer.

"He used you, brother. I know the feeling."

Tension filled the space between Kyle and Steven.

"Did you ask yourself, why would Victor have to kidnap his own daughter?"

"That's funny, Dad asked me the same thing and I'll tell you what I told him, she's not his daughter."

"What are you talking about?"

"If what Karina told me is true, this is big, and the only person I can trust is you."

Both Steven and Kyle looked back over their shoulders in the direction of their father then Kyle looked his brother right in the eye. "Are you telling me Dad is involved?"

"I don't know anything for sure but Karina

mentioned something that may have connected Dad to Pankov. Something that happened a long time ago."

"Back when we were kids?"

Steven started running what he thought he knew in his mind and he didn't like where it was going.

Kyle became anxious. "Think Steven. What makes the most sense?"

Steven took another hard look at his father. "This is going to have to stay between you and me. If this gets out, this could get real messy, real fast."

Kyle had never seen his younger brother lose his faith in their father before. When Kyle had joined the force, Steven had taken to wanting to be just like his father, and follow his older brother to join the force as well. That one thing became the only thing they all had in common, the badge.

"Is dad involved?"

To avoid Kyle's questions, Steven asked one of his own. "Your laptop, does it have a way to track a homing signal?"

"It's what I use to track some of my snitches, among other things. Why?"

"If I give you a frequency can you track it?"

"Sure, but—" Kyle caught a movement out of the corner of his eye. "Get ready, here comes Dad."

The eldest Morrell approached his boys, his gait projecting a purpose. The anticipated stress creating new, deep crevices in his face. He stared briefly at Kyle, then at Steven.

"You can't trust your brother, Steven," said the Captain.

"He's family," the youngest son replied.

"So?" the Captain countered.

"So are you, Dad. Based on what went on today, how can I trust you?"

A deep shade of red circled Captain Morrell's neck and rose to his cheeks. "And just how do you think Kyle can help you?"

"You should know that being an undercover officer, he has eyes and ears all over this city. I need all the help I can get to find Oksana. Plus, I wanted you to give Kyle the frequency of the pin you've been tracking."

"No."

"Why not?"

"Yeah, why not?" Kyle asked

"I see you haven't changed." Captain Morrell got a whiff of Kyle and mumbled under his breath, "Literally." He then told his boys to follow him to the staging area.

Kyle grabbed his laptop from the car and the two brothers followed their father to a small outdoor area sectioned off as a command center. At one of the tables, an officer sat with his laptop. On the screen was a grid with a red dot that seemed to appear and disappear in a sporadic fashion.

"Williams, give the tracking frequency to my son," the Captain ordered.

The junior officer typed a few keystrokes before relaying the information to Kyle. The father looked at his sons a long minute before saying, "Hope you know what you're getting yourselves into, boys."

As Kyle waited for his program to come online, he asked his brother, "So, who does this signal belong to?"

Steven answered, "Most top officials these days have a locator ID."

"So, who does the signal belong to?"

For the third time, Steven refused to answer Kyle.

Captain Morrell's officer said, "The ID belongs in the political arena. It's kind of a gray area."

"No," Steven said. "It doesn't get much more black-and-white than this."

Chapter 8

A plain white van with painted windows pulled up beside a black sedan parked in a quiet alley a short distance from the Vintage Hotel. A muscular Asian man opened the van's back door. Oksana lay bound and gagged beneath a dirty tarp on the floor. Her muted screams went unnoticed as two men from the sedan pulled her out of the van and dropped her into the trunk of the car.

Overwhelmed by grief and terror, Oksana lay absolutely still for what seemed like an interminable amount of time. Finally, she managed to pull one end of the duct tape from her mouth. After taking a deep breath, Oksana maneuvered the flag pin in her clenched hand. She kept opening and closing the switch on the back of the pin. Not sure if the locating signal still worked, the adolescent teenager prayed it did as she softly cried for her dead mother.

*****

Kyle was short with Captain Morrell's junior officer who was taking too long to gain access to the frequency. "Thanks, I got it from here."

As the officer walked away from the task at hand he crossed paths with his Captain, "What's his problem?"

The Captain replied, "Me."

*****

Steven moved in closer to his brother to observe the program running on his laptop.

Kyle glanced at his sibling as he said, "Don't let this get personal. Don't let them get to you."

Steven acknowledged with a nod of his head.

"What are you going to do?"

"Whatever it takes, Kyle."

"Now you're talking my language. Who are we going after and how deep does it go?"

"It's not how deep, but how high," answered Steven.

"Yeah?"

"Let's just say Dalton was caught in a compromising situation fifteen years ago and . . ."

Kyle finished his sentence, "The net result is he has a daughter no one knows about."

Cautiously, Steven looked around, before he nodded in response.

"How sure are you about this?"

Steven pointed out to Kyle the red blood stains on his shirt from Karina. "A hundred percent, brother."

Kyle's laptop beeped. The program picked up the signal of Oksana's pin.

*****

Masato Enterprises' warehouse occupied several blocks in Portland, Oregon's business district. Its owner, Ichiro Masato, fed the greedy mouths of politicians and local police. This allowed his empire to remain immune to city regulations while other businesses were not. Sins more wicked than tax evasion and fraud bloomed and thrived within the walls of his world.

The sedan transporting Oksana pulled up to a large roll-up garage door of Masato's warehouse. Two honks of the horn and the door opened. The vehicle drove in and the door closed behind it.

Oksana listened closely to the voices and activities coming from outside the car. Not sure what to expect, she slipped the flag pin into the pocket of her blue jeans.

One of the back doors of the sedan opened and two armed Asian men removed a large wooden crate from the back seat.

The box was stamped on each side with PROPERTY OF MASATO ENTERPRISES and a logo of a tiger's head branded beneath the Masato name.

The men removed the lid from the container and pulled out the thick layers of packing material. On a nearby table, they set out the contents of the box. It was an ornately carved stand displaying a Samurai sword.

Known as a katana, this exquisitely hand-carved masterpiece was considered as much art as it was a weapon. The handle of this particular sword was 12 inches of bone white ivory with the head of a roaring tiger carved into the handle.

After a few moments of admiring the priceless object, one of the men turned, looked up and nodded at the woman standing on the steel catwalk above them. Her expression was masked by the geisha makeup she wore.

Aiko, no longer the child but now a highly skilled geisha in full servitude, turned from the men below and knocked on a door to her right.

"Come."

Aiko carefully entered Masato's expensively furnished office. The slim, well-built Japanese businessman was sitting at his desk sipping a beer.

He was surrounded by a symbol he considered a representation of himself, the tiger. Behind him, hanging on the wall, was a large mural of a white Bengal Tiger. On his expansive cherry wood desk sat a bronze lamp in the form of a tiger. Even the wooden armrests of his office chair had tiger etchings on them.

Aiko entered the room as Masato was looking at a program on his laptop. The program showed four separate maps: North America, South America, Europe, and Japan. Each map had a series of red dots randomly scattered across its landscape. When Aiko approached his desk, he closed the laptop.

"The package has arrived," Aiko said as she bowed her head, a sign of respect for her master.

"It can wait." The fifty-two-year-old man finished his glass of beer, taking what was left in the bottle and poured it into the empty glass.

He motioned to the lovely geisha to come close to him.

The business tycoon stood up from his desk. One of his hands caressed Aiko on her shoulder. She squeezed her eyes shut and made fists as Masato walked behind her. His strong arms pulled her body into his, he slid them down and wrapped them around her waist.

Masato maneuvered his rough hand upward, sliding it back up along her sensuous body and inside his concubine's blue, silk kimono to fondle her breast.

"My precious, Aiko," Masato cooed in her ear.

Aiko knew her master could feel the tension throughout her body. Fully recognizing she would have to give in, Aiko exhaled a deep breath. Her body surrendered and the pressure in her hands released as contempt flowed through her veins.

Masato's left hand grabbed onto the end of the silk belt of her kimono. He wrapped his fingers around it before slowly pulling the tension out of the knot. Aiko's kimono fell open, exposing Masato's right hand caressing her left breast. He felt Aiko's heart pounding, sending his heart into a race with hers. As adrenaline ran through Masato's body, his desires for her awakened to new heights.

His hunger for Aiko was raw as he slipped the kimono off her shoulder, exposing the black-and-white stripes of her tiger tattoo. The tattoo was so perfect it looked as if it was growing right out of the geisha's flawless, tender-to-the-touch skin.

As wide as her shoulder blades at the top, the tattoo ran down the full length of her back in the shape of a V, the point ending at the small of her back.

Masato's mouth watered as he kissed her bare shoulder. Turning her towards the desk, Aiko reached out and braced herself. Masato squatted down behind her and reached up under her kimono, feeling the silky smoothness of her gorgeous legs. As his hands caressed their way up, he felt the edge of her panties and the heat radiating from within. After he stood, he bent Aiko over the desk. Her hands slid out in front of her across the top of the desk, knocking over the lamp and sending the empty beer bottle crashing to the floor.

The next sound was of a zipper being unzipped. Masato pulled her kimono away not only exposing her, but her one-of-a-kind tattoo. With one hand, he pulled her panties to the side and with the other hand, and with a sense of urgency, Masato thrust himself inside Aiko.

The tension, the pressure and the pain were almost more than the young woman could bear. Her silent screams choked her.

At first, Masato's touch to her spine was soft and tender as the palm of his hand slid up and down. It was as if his fingers were running through the fur of her tattoo. When his desire became more urgent, and the pounding fiercer, Masato gripped her back as if trying to grab the fur of this wild animal and tame it. His nails dug into her skin, leaving welts and drawing blood.

Aiko's feelings were revealed in the glass in front of her face. Her reflection distorted and twisted with every wave the beer made in the glass. With one final thrust from Masato, the glass fell over, spilling the rest of the beer. Aiko quickly lifted herself away from the spreading liquid.

When the tortuous ordeal for Aiko ended, Masato instructed her to clean up the office and herself then join him downstairs.

Using cleaning supplies from the executive bathroom, Aiko made sure the office was as pristine as possible. She quickly washed herself using a washcloth, noticing the bruising had already started to form on the front of her thighs where she was pressed against the desk.

She fixed her makeup and then put a small amount of salve on her palms where her fingernails had dug into her clenched fists.

Downstairs, Masato joined his men and, as he entered the room, his presence demanded respect and obedience. Command without question. He pulled his lead enforcer, Hitashi, to the side, "What about the two girls who got away?"

"They have been dealt with," Hitashi responded.

"How?"

Chapter 9

It was an absolutely perfect day to have the convertible top down. The wind twisted the long hair of two girls skyward as the sun warmed their tanned shoulders. Loud music surrounded Amber and Josie like a second skin. They felt almost invincible as they drove the black 2012 BMW convertible, capturing the attention of the people in vehicles around them.

*****

A foul mood filled every pore of the truck driver's body, causing him to become careless as he sped down the highway. Before he knew it, the driver found himself on the tail end of a black BMW convertible with two young ladies in it. When Amber realized the huge truck was inches from her bumper, she moved over from the left lane she was in, to the right lane. Just as the truck was equal to their car, a gust of wind caused it to momentarily drift into their lane, forcing Amber to move more to the right. The car's right-side tires went off the pavement onto the shoulder.

For a few seconds, Amber lost control. She was able to get it back on the highway, narrowly missing a REST AREA AHEAD sign.

Panic plastered the faces of Amber and Josie. Trying to get away from the truck, Amber sped up. "You believe this guy?" She laid on the horn a few times.

"Don't piss him off!" Josie shouted at Amber.

"I didn't do anything! He's crazy!" The frightened driver pushed the gas pedal of the car even farther to the floor. The BMW was nearly past the semi when one of the truck's tires exploded. The driver was unable to control his swaying truck and it clipped the back bumper of the BMW.

The car went into a sideways skid, fishtailed, and then slammed into six yellow barrels that were set out in the shape of a triangle at the split of the off-ramp that led to the rest area. As the barrels exploded on impact, water came down on the girls like a massive rainstorm. They screamed and closed their eyes. Then they felt it, something other than water. The smell was awful and their eyes stung from the vapors. There was a simultaneous gasp as the girls saw the slime that covered their bodies.

When they were able to finally open their eyes, Amber and Josie were horrified at the image in front of them.

It initiated even longer and louder screams than the ones before; a rotting corpse on the hood of the BMW, the decaying flesh hanging in threads off its bones.

Unable to open the car doors to get out, the girls turned to climb into the back seat when more blood-curdling screams erupted as they came face-to-face with a second corpse, in the same condition as the first one, sitting in the back seat.

*****

Masato approved of the report Hitoshi had given him about the girls. Only one more question needed to be clarified concerning the incident. Masato asked, "And what about the reporter with the black horn-rimmed glasses who convinced them to talk?"

*****

Within the hour, the area around the accident had been secured. Several patrol cars, a CSI unit, a tow truck and a coroner's car had blocked the highway causing traffic to be backed up for miles. Onlookers from the rest area were held back by crime scene tape and law enforcement.

Amber and Josie were huddled in blankets in the back of an ambulance, the EMTs treating them for shock.

In another barrel, its lid slightly knocked loose, an officer found an empty plastic jug marked POOL ACID floating on the surface of the rancid water. He reached for it and just before he touched it, a third corpse rose slowly to the surface. This shocked the officer into taking a step back. He regained his composure, peered over the edge of the barrel and saw the corpse wearing black horn-rimmed glasses. She had suffered the same fate as Masato's girls who believed talking to the reporter was going to make a difference.

The officer keyed his walkie-talkie... "We have another one!"

*****

Masato nodded in agreement. As he listened to his enforcer, he couldn't take his eyes off the katana, the majestic sword known as, The Guardian.

"Make sure the other girls understand what happened, and what will take place if they too decide to get any ideas about leaving."

Masato moved closer to the sword to get a better look at it. As he admired his acquisition, Aiko walked into the fold, absolutely stunning as a geisha in full makeup and kimono. To show respect, she lowered her eyes.

"I did not think I would own anything more beautiful than you, Aiko, but here it is, the Guardian. What do you think?"

"It is legendary."

"Yes, it is, and what about the key?" Masato demanded.

"Knowledge is the key."

"You've had time to study the sword, and what have you discovered?"

Aiko was silent.

"I sent you to the finest schools and have made the best training available to you, and your answer to me is silence?"

Masato removed the Guardian from its stand then pulled the sword from its protective sleeve, known as a scabbard. He ran the backside of the blade along Aiko's kimono and with a flick of his wrist, severed the belt. The kimono fell open leaving the cleavage of one of her ample breasts exposed.

The men looked away . . . all but one. Masato turned to the man and put the tip of the blade on his right cheek below his eye.

"Do not look at her. If I see you looking her in the eye again, that will be the last thing you ever see." Masato leaned in closer to the man's face, "Am I clear?"

The frightened look in the man's eyes said he understood. Masato leaned back, the tip of the blade still resting on his cheek. With another flick of his wrist, Masato gave the man a reminder, a slice diagonally down across his cheek. The man flinched but did not cry out.

"Just so we have an understanding," Masato said coldly. He then placed the sword on the man's other cheek.

"There is a key," Aiko announced.

Masato lowered the blade and walked over next to his mistress. Once again, he examined the well-preserved antique before him. Aiko noticed the one word of ancient Japanese language on it, known as Kojiki. On either side of the word, the symbols of Yin-Yang. Each Yin-Yang symbol had the black half of yin on top and the white half of yang on the bottom.

Aiko pointed to the stand. "This is the key. This tells us where the other sword is."

Waving the sword and strutting around the room, Masato's arrogance was at its highest. "You see gentlemen, this is not the sword I am looking for. This is the Guardian. This sword was commissioned for a great samurai warrior, my ancestor Kioshi Masato. What I am looking for is its companion sword, the tanto.

It's a one-of-a-kind masterpiece, fit for an emperor. As such, your eyes don't have the right to look upon its glory."

As Masato made his speech to his men, Aiko looked closer at the ancient hieroglyphic letters along the base of the stand. She ran her fingers along the letters and one of the yin-yang symbols. Careful not to reveal her emotions, Aiko had figured out where the second sword was.

"It is here." Aiko turned to face her Master. Her kimono was still loose, revealing her cleavage.

It was only a quick glance from the recently cut man, but that was all the excuse Masato needed to send a message to his men. In one swift motion, the sword removed the man's head. Drops of blood from the sword's tip landed on Aiko's chest and chalk-white face.

While their boss returned to the sword stand, Masato's men removed the body and severed head.

Too afraid to remove the blood from her own body, Aiko stood perfectly still while Masato removed his black tie and used it as a belt to hold her kimono shut.

"Now tell me, Aiko, where is the second sword?"

Experience and an intimate knowledge of Masato's personality had taught Aiko that once her angry boss had what he wanted, the deliverer of the package was considered an expendable threat. Fearing for her life, Aiko believed telling Masato where to find the sword would end her life.

"This stand is the key." Aiko pointed to it. "The swordsmith also made the stand. This is the companion piece."

Frustration quickly infuriated Masato and he threw his female possession to the floor, yelling in her face, "What are you saying?"

Barely able to speak, a trembling Aiko answered, "There is no second sword. It is the journey."

"Aaaaahhhhh," Masato released a primal scream as he raised the sword above her head. On her hands and knees, prepared to die, Aiko looked at the floor, her neck exposed for the fate that awaited her.

Just before the sword came down, the silence in the warehouse was interrupted by a faint knocking coming from the trunk of the sedan. Masato stepped back from his prey and put the sword back in the scabbard. Not realizing she had stopped breathing, Aiko drew in the tiniest breath of air.

Masato turned and asked one of his men, "I see our new arrival is ready to come out and play."

"Yes, Master."

"Bring her to me."

The sedan driver popped the trunk open and two men pulled Oksana out. She momentarily shut her eyes to protect them from the bright lights.

Standing before Masato, was a girl showing the first signs of womanhood. The thick natural curls of her dark brown hair cascaded down Oksana's back. Her large brown eyes were framed by long black eyelashes. She scanned the scene before her, observing an oddly dressed woman on her hands and knees, and smartly dressed men standing rigidly near an older man with a dangerous smile on his face.

"Your father was right, you will bring a good price." Masato stepped forward and gently touched the frightened girl's cheek.

"He is not my father," Oksana vehemently replied as she stepped back from Masato's fingers. "I heard him say that I will bring trouble to you."

This statement amused Oksana's captor, so he asked, "And why is that, little one?"

"My father is President Dalton, not Victor Pankov."

Masato laughed and replied, "Well, then. Your price just went up, Ms. Dalton." He was about to engage in further conversation with the feisty teenager when one of his men stationed outside, approached him.

"There's a car down the block with two men in it, Master. I am unsure at this time who they are, but their vehicle is the type used in law enforcement for undercover work."

"They're probably here for me," Oksana blurted out.

Turning to the rest of his men, Masato began yelling out orders. "Take the girl to be with the others. Stay with her at all times. Get rid of the car and put the sword and its stand in my office, immediately." Masato pulled Aiko off the floor and hissed at her, "Stay with the sword and do not let it out of your sight."

Chapter 10

Outside the Masato warehouse, Steven and Kyle managed to get past the guards unnoticed and station themselves near one of the ground level windows on the side of the building. They watched in horror as Masato decapitated one of his own men.

Steven turned to Kyle, "What just happened?"

"Masato just happened," replied Kyle.

The detectives carefully moved away from the window and peeked around the corner of the building. Two FBI agents were standing by the trunk of their car putting on navy blue FBI windbreakers over their bulletproof vests. Steven and Kyle retreated to their original positions. In a voice barely above a whisper, they continued their conversation.

"Tell me more about Masato," Steven urged.

"He's behind a lot of things, none of it good. I've always had a feeling he had something to do with Mom's death. Somehow, Dad was either a part of it or Masato has something very incriminating on him."

"He just might have something," Steven said. "Karina mentioned Pankov has a file with Dad's name on it. Kyle, do you really believe Dad's been compromised?"

"I know these guys wouldn't have a file unless they had a reason to. And lately, some things just haven't been adding up."

"Who else you think is involved?"

"Don't know. The FBI and the Portland Police Department Task Force have been investigating Masato for years. But every time we get someone undercover into his organization, they disappear or turn up dead."

"Does any of this tie in with anything you're working on now?"

"No, Steven, but the latest word on the street is they made a merger of epic proportions a couple of years ago. There's Pankov, who you've probably figured out by now sells the girls on the black market and Masato, who exploits them on the Internet."

"And you think that maybe Dad has been tipping them off?"

"I guess the answer is in that file."

Steven stole another glance at the two FBI agents. "Now why would there be only two agents showing up here?"

A low, half laugh came from Kyle. "Don't know. Why are you and me here without back-up? It's because we're just observing."

"How did the FBI know we were here?"

"They didn't. They followed the same signal we did."

"Don't we need a warrant?"

"I'm sure the feds have one. Once the shooting starts, we're good to go."

"Now what?"

"Well, more than likely they already know we're here." Kyle pointed to an exterior surveillance camera mounted on the wall above their position. He checked his gun and looked at Steven. "Ready?"

Steven rocked the slide on his automatic and made sure a round was in the chamber. "Ready."

On their way to meet up with the FBI agents, Steven gave the surveillance camera the universal one-fingered salute.

The movement of the brothers rounding the corner startled the FBI agents. Just as they reached for their weapons, Kyle immediately held up his identification.

"What the—?" one of the agents said.

"Detectives Steven and Kyle Morrell. We'll take the back, you guys take the front."

The brothers disappeared around the corner before either agent could say a word.

As Steven and Kyle approached the back entrance, one of the FBI agents looked in one of the front warehouse windows. The sound of a gunshot echoed and the agent fell over dead with a bullet hole in the middle of his forehead.

Just as Kyle and Steven prepared to go in, the large delivery bay door next to them rolled up. Once the door was high enough, the sedan that had transported Oksana sped out. The door then immediately closed. Kyle fired two rounds in the direction of the driver, killing him instantly. The car smashed into a retaining wall a short distance from the warehouse. A man in the front passenger seat jumped from the car and pointed his gun at Kyle. Steven got a round off first, taking the man down with one shot.

When the two brothers checked the car's trunk, Oksana was not in it. They quickly went back to the warehouse and slipped quietly through the back door. Nobody seemed to be around until they spotted a figure entering a door on the catwalk above them. Two silhouettes were briefly visible behind the semi-closed blinds on the front window of the office just before the lights in the room went out.

Kyle whispered to Steven that he was moving to the left side of the warehouse for a closer look. One of Masato's men stepped out from behind a stack of large crates with an assault rifle aimed at Kyle. Steven fired his gun at the man, hitting him in the chest. Bullets sprayed from the assailant's Mac-10 in the direction of the two detectives as the trigger-man went down. Another angle of the attack came from Masato on the catwalk, and more from a third man on the floor guarding the front entrance.

When Masato's handgun was empty, he stepped back into his office, opened a hidden wall cabinet, armed himself with a Mac-10, and grabbed another clip for his handgun.

"Looks like it's time for us to go," Masato said to Aiko. He grabbed her hand and just as they reached the door, bullets shattered the office window. The couple immediately flattened themselves against a wall behind the door. Masato waited for the gunfire to subside, then he checked the handgun making sure the clip was full and the safety was off before giving it to Aiko.

"Wait here, I will be back for you." Masato stood at the office doorway and yelled orders in Japanese.

The ammunition from his second gunman's assault rifle sprayed faster and more erratic than moments before, hitting everything around them. Pipes began hissing steam from ruptured hot water lines. Shattering the glass from the emergency fire hose case that was mounted on the wall behind them exploded, and the indiscriminate bullets seemed to rain down and ricochet like little metal spheres on a pinball machine. Masato took advantage of the chaos and fired his weapon into the fray as he exited the office, leaving Aiko behind.

Out-gunned, Kyle and Steven each headed in different directions in order to avoid the continuous spray of bullets. With their heads ducked, they didn't see Masato leave the office and come down the stairs from the catwalk.

Steven's cell phone vibrated in his pocket, the call was from Kyle.

"I'm pinned down here and running out of things to hide behind. Can you lay down some cover so I can make my way back to you?"

"It's not much better where I'm at, but if you can get over here, we might be able to get out through the back door."

"What happened to the two FBI agents we saw earlier?" Kyle asked.

"One of them has been hit and is down, over by the stairs. Not sure of his condition."

"And the second one?"

"I saw the other one down, just outside the entrance. He's definitely out of the picture," Steven said.

Steven and Kyle both put fresh clips in their Berettas.

"Cover me, I'm coming to you."

Steven began laying down cover fire, hitting one of the gunmen. As Kyle moved closer to his brother, he also fired and took out another one of Masato's men.

There was a short reprieve from the gunfire allowing the brothers to meet up.

"You have any idea how many are still out there?" asked Kyle.

"I took out one of them, hit another one, but I'm not sure if he's down. You got one on the way here, that leaves the two upstairs," replied Steven.

"Anything out of Mr. FBI?"

"As far as I can tell he's still alive, but I don't know for how long."

Steven saw the FBI agent trying to sit up. He started making his way toward the downed agent, but Kyle objected.

"Steven, wait." Kyle started to follow, but immediately drew fire from across the room, keeping him pinned down.

Meanwhile, Steven worked his way through the warehouse, using the stairs for cover. He nearly stumbled over one of Masato's men that he had taken out earlier. Relieving the dead man of his 9mm and assault rifle, Steven then checked the clip on the handgun before placing it in the front of his waistband. He continued toward the downed FBI agent until he was a few yards from him. The two men made eye contact.

Masato had been waiting patiently in the shadows. He surprised Steven from behind and pistol-whipped him. He was struck hard enough to make him drop the assault rifle, but not debilitating enough to make him completely lose his footing. The pain was blinding.

Despite the chaos around him, Kyle saw what happened to Steven. He cautiously made his way toward his brother. Once Kyle felt he was close enough a take a shot at Masato, he realized his adversary was using his brother as a shield.

Above them, the door to Masato's office opened. Kyle saw movement and a pistol pointed in his direction. He fired one shot into the open doorway.

The bullet ricocheted off the door, wounding Aiko. She was able to take one step through the door before falling to the floor of the catwalk.

Masato barely noticed what transpired above him. Instead, he kept a closer look on his hostage. It wasn't until Aiko softly cried out that he looked up and noticed her face through the steel grate of the catwalk. Intense pain showed in her eyes and contorted her face as she whispered, "Help me."

Masato laid down cover fire in Kyle's direction. The detective took cover behind some wooden crates.

Deciding to cut his losses, Masato took one last look at Aiko as he pointed his gun in her direction and fired. Recognizing his intention, Aiko tried to roll out of the way. The shot caught her in the side. An intense burning sensation made her press her hand tightly over the bullet wound at her waist. Blood trickled down between her fingers.

Masato walked backward, heading for the exit. Kyle had a clear shot of him, but the unscrupulous executive had his own clear shot of Steven standing dazed and helpless.

"Choose," Masato commanded.

"Shoot him, Kyle," Steven said with the same authority.

Masato pointed his gun at Steven's head. Steven stared hard at Kyle, who slowly moved his hand toward his waistband for the handgun he had tucked away.

"Not a good idea," Masato said as he shot the wounded FBI agent on the floor next to Steven, killing him instantly. He then trained his gun back on Steven. "Choose, Detective."

"Kyle, I'm sorry." Steven looked at his brother with deep regret in his eyes.

"It's okay, brother. If everybody just stays cool, we'll all go home."

Kyle gestured to Masato. "There's the door. Go." Kyle took a step back and began to set his gun down on a large crate of artwork.

A condescending look spread across Masato's face as he stepped backward, toward the rear door. "Like father like son. I see where you get your weakness."

"What's he talking about, Kyle?"

"Your father—" Masato said. But before he could finish his sentence, Steven reached for the 9mm in his waistband. Just as he drew it and took aim at Masato, the enemy let loose with the Mac-10. Steven was shot multiple times. The spray of bullets from the assault rifle sent Kyle ducking for cover.

As the dust settled, Kyle heard the back-door slam shut. He looked up and saw Masato had disappeared. On the floor, twisting in agony lay Steven. Kyle rushed over to him, dropped to his knees and took his dying brother in his arms.

Kyle's cries echoed through the empty warehouse. "Steven!" Kyle held his hands over Steven's bleeding chest.

His words barely a whisper, Steven said, "The file Dad had on Mom's accident wasn't…"

Kyle felt the life drain from his little brother's bullet-riddled body. In silence, he felt Steven's soul pass on. Looking toward the heavens, Kyle cried out, "God, please take care of him, he didn't deserve this."

Moments later, a drop of blood landed on Kyle's cheek. He looked up, trying to focus in on where it came from. Above him, he saw Aiko lying on her back on the steel grate of the catwalk. By now she had lost the strength to press firmly on her wound.

"Help me," she gasped. More blood dripped off her soaked kimono onto Kyle's shoulder. The last vision Aiko had before everything went black, was a pair of gorgeous green eyes with a mystified look in them.

Kyle checked the carotid artery on her neck for any signs of life. He felt a whisper of a pulse. Kyle could sense this woman was a fighter and there was no way he was going to give up on her. Especially if she was the only link that could lead him to the man who killed his brother in cold blood, Masato.

Kyle loosened his shirt and tore off enough of it to dress her wounds as best he could. He removed the satin belt from her kimono and used it as a tourniquet to hold the makeshift field dressing in place. A shot rang out from seemingly nowhere as it pinged off the handrail next to him. Kyle heard the *click* the empty handgun made as one of Masato's wounded men was pointing in Kyle's direction from the floor of the warehouse. Then a series of clicks as the man kept pulling the trigger, but to no avail.

As Kyle made his way down to the floor, he got on his phone and called in asking for two ambulances. One for the woman who he hoped could be of some use to him in finding his brother's killer and one for his brother who had his life cut short by a man who had no moral compass whatsoever. In the time it took for Kyle to reach the only surviving member of Masato's crew, Kyle had answered his own question,

"Once you find him; how do you arrest such a man? You don't ".

Kyle disarmed the dying gunman on the floor, pulled a clip from his own belt, reloaded the weapon, and then sent one round into the chamber.

The dying man's words rang true. "You can't kill me, I'm already dead."

Kyle pointed the gun at the man's forehead and replied in jest, "Then I guess you won't feel this."

The fallen man was prepared to die and closed his eyes. When nothing happened, he opened his eyes to see Kyle pacing.

Kyle was questioning himself, *"Did he have nothing to lose or maybe he did?"* He looked at the wounded gunman. "Tell me something. Why would your boss want to make sure you were all left for dead? There's got to be a bigger picture and I think you're the guy who's going to fill in the blanks. How does that sound?"

No response from the gunman who seemed to be fading fast from his wounds.

"How about we save your life first then after, we let Masato know you cooperated fully in our investigation, then we let you go? What do you think will happen to you then?"

"I'm a dead man either way."

"Yeah, that's true. How about we make a game of it anyway?"

Kyle grabbed a nearby chair and helped the gunman into it. "We need to get you a tourniquet." Kyle took hold of the back of the chair and dragged the man over to the wall near the entrance where the emergency fire hose was located. Kyle unraveled enough hose to wrap it around the man's torso enough times to fully encase it in the firehose. As he shoved the nozzle end of the hose in the loose portion behind the man's back, he asked him, "Okay, how does that feel?"

The gunman didn't find his humor amusing. "Tell me where Masato is and I'll let you die as you wish or I'll save you and leave it up to fate."

Still no reply from the stubborn man.

"Oh good. I'm glad you're not cooperating." Kyle saw blood dripping from the man onto the floor. "We better do something about that leak you have or you may not be any use to me at all."

Kyle reached over to the firebox and partially opened the valve just enough to start releasing the water. The man could feel the pressure from the hose begin to squeeze like an anaconda as it filled, squeezing him without mercy.

"You can tell me when you want me to stop

or you can just let me know by letting your eyes pop out. Either way, I'm in it for the long haul."

The pressure became so much the man had no room or ability to breath to give a clear response. He just began to jerk in the chair fighting the losing fight. Kyle turned off the water then pulled the end of the hose out and released the high-pressure fireman's nozzle releasing the torturous grip on the man. His lungs gasped for air as he could feel his blood start recirculating again. Both men could hear the sirens getting closer.

Kyle made an offer, "Last chance."

The man just mustered enough energy to gather up the blood in his mouth and spit it in Kyle's direction. Kyle tucked the nozzle back into its snug hiding place. "Really? After all I've done for you by saving your worthless life."

"My God has a place for me."

"I guess we'll see if that's true."

Kyle knew the ambulance was only minutes out so as he walked out the entrance to greet the E.M.S bus. When he did, he threw the handle to the water valve wide open.

Chapter 11

Groggy and confused, the young woman slowly opened her eyes and surveyed her surroundings. Minutes passed before Aiko understood she was in a hospital room. The white geisha makeup had been removed from her face and her long, black hair lay fanned out across her pillow. A heart monitor steadily beeped next to her bed. Antiseptic vapors drifted in her nostrils, the dimmed fluorescent lights were harsh and the hospital bed next to hers was empty. Mounted to the wall across from Aiko's bed was a muted TV with the closed caption option on. She read the crawl at the bottom of the screen. "Breaking news. Sources confirm that the summit hearings between the Russian Prime Minister and The President of the United States are still on hold at this time."

*****

Kyle absently thumbed through magazines while he and Officer Pena sat in the hallway outside of Aiko's room at Portland Memorial Hospital.

His mind shuffled back and forth between the dying faces of his brother and that of the frightened eyes of a geisha begging for help.

The pieces to this unsolved puzzle were increasing by the hour. Kyle tried to concentrate on nothing and everything at the same time. Doctor Turner, Aiko's physician, walked up to the nurses' station. Kyle intercepted him and asked, "How is she?"

"Well, she lost a lot of blood, but it looks like it will be a full recovery. She needs plenty of bed rest and non-strenuous activity for at least a week," Doctor Turner replied. "Did you find out what her name is yet?"

"No, but we did run her fingerprints. She isn't in our system."

Kyle hoped Turner hadn't noticed when he caught himself not listening to the doctor, but thinking of Aiko.

"We're already running a blood panel, maybe we can find something in the CODIS database."

"What else can you tell me about her...her condition, I mean?"

Kyle's cheeks became flush as a result of his embarrassment at his exposed feelings for Aiko. He wasn't sure if the doctor had picked up on it.

"The patient is in really good physical shape for her age, so recovery time for her should be better than for most. She's been through a lot of physical trauma. First, we sutured the wounds from the through and through on her lower right side and then removed the fragments of the 9mm from near the rib on her left side. Nothing major was hit so she should recover nicely."

Preoccupied with the information the doctor was explaining to him, Kyle didn't notice Officer Pena walk past him toward the hospital cafeteria.

"Two gunshots?"

"Yes, we recovered your 9mm that lodged just under the skin next to one of her ribs on the left, but the one that passed through on the right side looked to be of a different caliber. Neither would have been instantly fatal, but if you hadn't brought her in right away, she most likely would have bled out."

Kyle's mouth felt dry and thick. "I fired once in her direction. I hit the door then noticed she went down. The bullet must have ricocheted. I swear I only fired once in her direction."

"I believe you," said Doctor Turner. "The bullets were two different calibers."

"When I fired in her direction, I didn't see her. I just saw a gun pointing through the doorway above us."

"Any idea where that second shot came from?"

"There were so many bullets flying around, it could have come from anywhere. Can I talk to the girl? Maybe she can tell us."

Doctor Turner sighed, "She's no girl, Kyle. She's a young woman who as I mentioned earlier, has been through a lot more than just being shot. We found bruising throughout her body and scarring going back for years. There is also tearing that indicates she was sexually abused in the last 24 hours, so we will be running a rape kit as well."

The sour bile rising in Kyle's stomach was no longer from hunger, lack of sleep or the recent whirlwind of activity. It was a combination of an anger born from Karina's death, Oksana's disappearance, Steven's death and now the revelations of an abused stranger.

His thoughts were interrupted by Doctor Turner. "You can talk to her if she's awake. If not, let her sleep. She needs it."

"Okay, doc. Thanks for everything."

"No problem. And Kyle, I'm sorry to hear about your brother. Your father is in the mortuary talking to the coroner about the arrangements for Steven if you want to join him."

Kyle looked briefly at the elevators and decided he wasn't ready to deal with his father. Instead, he turned and walked down the hallway toward Aiko's room.

*****

Tired beyond description, Aiko had closed her eyes. She didn't know how long she had slept before she felt a presence next to her bed. She assumed it was a nurse or doctor checking on her. Suddenly, she felt the strength of a man's hand over her mouth. Her eyes flew open, terror paralyzed her entire body. Dressed as a doctor, Masato stood over her and as their eyes met, Aiko knew this was no longer the man who raised her. The tenderness he had once shown to her was gone and had been replaced by indifference. She saw the tiger that was in his soul and he acted like there was no cage that could keep him from being the animal that he truly was. An animal that would rather die than be imprisoned. Masato motioned for her to be quiet.

He slowly removed his hand and she attempted to scream.

This time when he put his hand over her mouth, he pressed the edge of his hand up to her nose cutting off her breathing. Aiko felt what he always had over her, the will to do as he wished without any regard for human life. She nodded, and he let her breathe.

Masato took a piece of gauze and stuffed it into her mouth. "I need the truth from you, Aiko."

Aiko knew he would not stop even if she gave him everything he wanted to hear. The problem was the truth did not matter to him. Aiko tried to reach up and pull the gauze out of her mouth but all she ended up doing was to pull out the I.V. that had been attached to the back of her hand.

Masato grabbed her wrist and pulled it back down with authority. With one hand, he clutched both her hands and with the other he reached inside the set of scrubs he was wearing and produced two police issued plastic ties that were used as handcuffs. He attached her wrists, one at a time, to the side rails of the bed.

Masato then reached over and removed the blood pressure cuff from the basket on the wall. Aiko looked on in horror as he put it around her neck and secured the fit.

He then closed the valve on the bp cuff and began to slowly squeeze the bulb, adding air to tighten the cuff, thereby cutting off her air supply. The Velcro on the cuff began to crackle as it fought to stay connected.

The beeps of the EKG machine attached to her vitals intensified. Masato leaned down close to her ear and spoke low, but harshly to her, "What have you told them?"

Aiko's terrified brown eyes filled with tears. Masato pulled the gauze out of her mouth and released the valve reducing the pressure around her neck. She took in deep breaths through her nose.

"I have said nothing, Master," Aiko gasped.

Masato closed the valve with his thumb and slowly squeezed the bulb once again, tightening the blood pressure cuff around the young woman's throat. Echoes of her heartbeat raced faster on the EKG machine.

Masato's voice was still fierce as he questioned her. "Have you told them your name? He released the valve allowing Aiko a few precious breaths of air. The monitoring of the EKG machine slowly returned to normal sinus rhythm with each nourishing breath.

She swallowed hard. "No, nothing—" Her sentence was cut off by Masato's words.

"You know how much I love you, my little one. You must realize how difficult this is for me."

Masato closed the valve with his thumb and slowly squeezed the bulb, tightening the cuff once again. With each squeeze of the bulb, it choked Aiko and the Velcro dug deeper and deeper into her skin.

Kyle entered Aiko's room just as he heard Masato say, "My little one." Thinking it odd that a doctor would address a patient in this manner, Kyle walked toward the man leaning over Aiko's bed. He was shocked by what he saw. The dull gray BP cuff was fully inflated around Aiko's neck, choking the life out of her. Suddenly, he understood why her EKG monitor's beeps were getting quicker by the second.

Without warning, Masato threw an elbow into Kyle's face knocking him backward. While the two men fought, Aiko struggled for air. Unable to do anything, she slipped herself into a semi-conscious meditative state, lowering her own heart rate through a form of an ancient meditation. With her remaining strength, Aiko pulled at the plastic cuffs that restrained her to the bed. The plastic ripped into the skin on her wrists.

Masato's fighting style far outmatched Kyle's. The martial arts expert landed a punch so solid to the detective's chest it knocked the wind out of him, sending him backward into the cabinets. As Kyle fell to his knees, he reached out for the counter. One hand grabbed a metal pan off the counter and the other hung onto a drawer handle. As he went to the floor, the drawer came flying out, emptying its contents of surgical instruments onto the ground.

When Masato attempted to kick his weaker opponent, Kyle blocked his leg and smashed the metal pan on the inside of Masato's knee. This gave Kyle the time he needed to stand and get back into the fight. The two men exchanged another set of punches, but this time Kyle connected with the metal pan to the side of Masato's head, just above his eye, leaving a small gash. Trace amounts of Masato's blood stained the side of the pan.

As Masato's momentum took him into the wall, he grabbed onto the waste syringe box. As he tried to steady himself, he ripped the plastic box open. Used syringes fell out onto the floor but a handful remained in the bottom of the box. Masato gripped as many as he could and came at Kyle with a series of used needles like they were mini daggers.

As Masato turned, he threw the syringes at Kyle One happened to find its target and stuck into Kyle's neck. Before Kyle could pull it out, Masato was on him and his momentum took them both to the ground in a heap. Kyle had Masato's left arm pinned but only had Masato's right hand by the wrist with his left. Masato could see the syringe's plunger was not all the way down and had an air bubble in the tube. He tried to use his strength over Kyle to reach for the syringe and force down the plunger. Kyle's only choice was to let go of Masato's left arm and take a swing at him. He connected with a solid blow that rocked Masato back. Kyle got a leg between them and was able to kick Masato off of him. Masato's body slid back across the floor toward the door.

Aiko's EKG monitor had reached its limit and the alarm had just gone off. The distraction was enough for Masato to take advantage of the situation and rushed out of the room and down the hall.

Kyle was careful to remove the needle from his neck. He then forced himself to get up and rush to Aiko's side where he ripped the bp cuff off her neck. Checking for a pulse, he found one so faint it was barely noticeable.

He immediately started a form of CPR known as rescue breathing, giving her two quick breaths to see if she would respond.

Nurse Nancy Carter entered Aiko's room following the alarm that alerted her at the nurse's station. The room was in disarray and a man, not a doctor, was leaning over her patient. She said loudly, "What in God's name is going on here?"

Chapter 12

"Get a doctor, now!", Nurse Carter's plea could be heard as she scurried out of the room. "Somebody just tried to kill this woman!"

Kyle continued his efforts to resuscitate Aiko.

"Come on, wake up." Kyle pleaded. He grabbed a pair of surgical scissors from off the floor and cut the plastic handcuffs from Aiko's wrists. Just as he freed her second wrist, Aiko came back to life with a vengeance. The sudden gasp of air that filled her lungs also filled her body with animation. In an unexpected reflex, she sat up and wrapped her arms around Kyle. Unsure what else to do, he let her hang onto him, allowing her to feel the safety of his arms.

When Kyle felt her start to relax, he carefully laid her back down on the bed. They gazed into each other's eyes. It was then that Aiko recognized the same green eyes of the man who must have saved her on the catwalk.

Kyle gently asked, "What's your name?"

"Aiko."

"Why does—" Kyle's questioning was interrupted by Doctor Turner, Captain Morrell, and Officer Pena's hurried entrance into the room.

"What's going on here?" The doctor demanded as he immediately went to Aiko's side to examine her.

Able to let his guard down because Doctor Turner was tending to Aiko, Kyle spoke to his dad and Officer Pena. "Masato was trying to kill Aiko."

"Aiko?" Captain Morrell repeated.

"Yeah, her name is Aiko."

Kyle returned his gaze to the young woman lying in the hospital bed. Despite her disheveled appearance and lack of makeup, she was naturally alluring and very exotic.

"Does she have a last name?"

"We haven't gotten that far yet."

Captain Morrell turned to Pena. "How did Masato get past you?"

"I didn't know it was Masato. He was dressed as a doctor requesting the room to do an examination. I took a couple of minutes to go get some coffee when I—"

The anger in Captain Morrell's face told Pena not to bother finishing his explanation. Kyle has seen this anger in his father before and decided to change the subject.

"Dad," Kyle said halfheartedly. "I heard you were here taking care of arrangements for Steven."

Sadness had rolled over Captain Morrell's face like the dark gray clouds of a pending storm. "Yeah, I got that all taken care of. After talking with the coroner, he said he had a few questions about what happened. I agreed with him and came up to this floor looking for you. I had just made it to the nurse's station when I saw Dr. Turner and Pena headed this way."

As Dr. Turner examined Aiko, Kyle pulled his father to the side.

"It was Masato, I'm sure of it. When I came in here, he had the BP cuff around her neck and plastic Zip Ties strapping her to the bed."

"Well, Aiko," Doctor Turner said with a smile. "It's nice to finally know your name."

Her throat still sore from the fresh strangulation attempt, Aiko nodded at the doctor.

"Now, gentlemen," the doctor said with gravity. "Aiko needs at least a week to get back on her feet without someone trying to kill her. Is having an around-the-clock guard by her room too much to ask?"

"I think I'm going to take her to a safe house rather than worry about security issues here," Kyle said.

"That's not a good idea. She still needs to be monitored, especially after this last incident," Doctor Turner insisted.

"Look doc, I'll bring her back in a few days so you can examine her, I promise." Kyle watched Aiko out of the corner of his eye.

"I want it on record that I don't think this is a good idea."

"I'll put it on record," Kyle acknowledged. "Dad, remember the place that Steven and I spent with you after Mom died? I can take her there."

Captain Morrell paused before answering, "Yeah, good choice son."

"And just where is this place?" Doctor Turner asked.

"I'll tell you before we leave the hospital. But for now, we need to figure out how to get Aiko out of here without being seen," Kyle said.

"I'm sure Masato has men watching the hospital," Captain Morrell added.

Kyle touched Aiko's hand. "Aiko, do Masato's men know you only as a geisha?"

"Yes."

"Are you sure?"

"Yes, I am sure."

*****

Nurse Carter walked ahead of the gurney. She reached back and pulled the stretcher down the hall, clearing obstructions as she went. The second nurse carefully steered from the back.

Just as they exited the emergency doors, two Asian men walked up to the gurney and bumped it, stopping its momentum. One of the men lifted the sheet and observed a Caucasian man with his head wrapped in bandages.

"What do you think you're doing?" snapped Nurse Carter. "It's imperative we get this man in the ambulance. Please get out of our way."

The two Asian men looked at each other and then at Nurse Carter. Seeing she would not hesitate to call for assistance, they left. Once the gurney was in the ambulance with the doors closed, Nurse Carter turned to the other nurse and laughed, "Well, what do you think, Ms. Aiko?"

Masato's men were so focused on who might be under the sheet on the gurney, they never noticed it was Aiko with her hair down, no makeup, and in full scrubs steering the gurney. The gurney was also useful in assisting her to walk right out of the hospital in plain sight.

Aiko raised her head and looked at Nurse Carter, then bowed her head as a gesture of thanks, but found it hard to focus.

She removed the glasses she was wearing.

"Honey, I'm going to need my glasses back so I can get on with finishing my rounds."

The grateful patient handed the glasses back to Nurse Carter. She then removed a surgical cap and a surgical mask that she had hanging around her neck to hide the bruises from the BP cuff and handed them to Carter.

"Thank you for your assistance, Nurse Carter."

Kyle sat up on the gurney and removed the bandages from his head. "We really appreciate your help in getting Aiko out safely."

"No problem, handsome. Anytime, for you," Carter said as she winked at Kyle.

After Carter left, Captain Morrell climbed into the cab of the ambulance and looked back at Aiko. "Are you ready for a little vacation?"

Not waiting for an answer, he put the ambulance in gear and headed north in the direction of Jantzen Beach.

Chapter 13

Conversation between Kyle and Aiko had been scarce since they left the hospital. The ambulance had taken them to another hospital across town, where the two of them got out and called for a taxi. They had the driver drop them off at a Target store where they bought some personal items and clothing. From there, they called another taxi and twenty-five minutes later, arrived at the east end of Hayden Island. Rows of houseboats moored to the docks lined the river's edge. Kyle paid the driver and carried their packages toward one of the houseboats. Aiko walked beside him, her arm hooked around his to help keep herself steady.

The reflection from a rich red sunset rode the small choppy waves of the wide channel, an offshoot of the Columbia River. This part of the river separated Hayden Island from the mainland. The brilliant colors of the evening sky seemed to be a gift painted just for Aiko. She could not remember the last time she was outside. Sounds and smells nearly forgotten to her sheltered senses, now opened for her like a new blossom.

Kyle slowed his pace to help Aiko make her way along a weathered and narrow dock.

It didn't take long before they were standing before a rustic, two-bedroom houseboat. Strands of small lights in the shape of icicles were attached to the edge of the roof, left over from Christmas by the previous guest. The deck was partially covered by a tin overhang which helped protect a large, green couch. A couple of faded plastic lawn chairs were set up on the exposed part of the wooden deck.

"It's not much Aiko, but we should be safe here," Kyle said, his uncertainty pushed beneath his confident exterior.

"Does your family own this place?"

"It belongs to a friend of my Dad's. Her name is Alicia. They've known each other for years. She runs Davenport Real Estate. They manage and rent out a lot of the houseboats in this area for absent owners. She happens to own this one."

"This is a nice place. Your friend is very kind for letting us stay here. Thank you for bringing me here."

Aiko did not think she remembered how to smile, but this place brought the slightest upward curve to the corners of her mouth, an expression she tried to hide from Kyle.

It had been a long two days for the couple. Kyle checked the refrigerator and found only bottled water and condiment packets leftover from previous fast food runs. When he closed the door, he saw a magnet advertising Pisano's Pizza. He used his cell phone to order a pizza to be delivered. While Kyle was on the phone, Aiko wandered the houseboat, surveying her surroundings.

After checking out the main living quarters, Aiko went into the master bedroom and closed the door. Carefully taking off the scrubs, she put on a comfortable set of yoga pants and a top. In the bathroom, she washed her face, brushed her teeth and put her hair in a ponytail. Staring at herself in the mirror, Aiko lightly touched her bruised neck. She held her raw emotions in check, especially those from the knowledge that her life was insignificant to her master. He would rather kill her before allowing her to talk to the police. When she looked past the barrel of the gun, just before he pulled the trigger, she saw an illusion of the man she used to know.

Returning to the kitchen, Aiko saw Kyle had laid out paper plates, napkins and a couple of glasses.

"The pizza will be here in about 30 minutes. I'm afraid we'll have to make do with bottled water tonight. Tomorrow, I'll go shopping. Anything special you like to eat?"

"I prefer fresh vegetables, rice, and fresh seafood. Do you like to fish, Kyle?"

"Love it. We used to come here when I was a kid and catch fish right off the back of the deck."

Talk between Aiko and Kyle stayed limited to short impersonal sentences. Their confused emotions were awkward for both of them. They ate their pizza mostly in silence. Aiko used a fork and knife while Kyle used his hands. Almost immediately after their meal, exhaustion overtook them with a vengeance. A polite goodnight and each headed off to their own rooms.

*****

Dancing sun particles circled around Aiko as she did stretching exercises in the living room. Kyle watched her from the laundry room door frame before he walked in with a small laundry basket of clothes.

"Doctor Turner said to take it easy for a full week, Aiko. It's only been five days."

"He does not know my body, only I do." She continued to bend her limbs in degrees Kyle didn't think was humanly possible.

"I still think—"

Kyle didn't finish his sentence. He felt Aiko's emotionless, black eyes boring into him.

"Hey, I have something for you." Kyle went to the hall closet and returned with a long cardboard box and a bag. He removed a pair of jeans from the bag and handed them to Aiko.

"Every Portland samurai needs her own pair of jeans."

Aiko gingerly ran her hands over the smooth cotton of the jeans. "I have never owned such a garment as these."

"Oh, I almost forgot." Kyle went back to the closet, took out a small shoebox and presented it to Aiko. "These are Vans."

Aiko looked in the box. "I've never owned a pair of tennis shoes either."

"These are different, these are Vans. They're like tennis shoes but without the laces. I thought you would like these because you're always asking me to remove my shoes when I enter the house, so I got a pair for each of us." Kyle smiled then said, "You can thank me later."

Aiko found that odd but took Kyle's statement at face value. Kyle opened the long box and removed the protective plastic wrap. Carefully he unwrapped the item and showed Aiko her gift.

It was a replica of a samurai sword. The 40-inch sword, known as a katana, was well made for being a reproduction.

As he held the sword out toward Aiko he said, "I believe this is what you were talking about the other night. It's the best I could find on short notice."

Aiko stood up in front of Kyle. "Two hands. Do you not respect me?"

It took a second for Kyle to understand what she meant. "Of course I respect you."

"Then use two hands when you give something to someone and slightly bow your head."

The message now clear, Kyle stood straight before Aiko and with a nod of his head, handed her the sword with both hands.

"Thank you, Kyle. Why would you do this for me?"

"When you told me how much the other sword meant to you and how you used to train with it, I thought I would try to find a replacement for you."

Aiko became more somber than usual when she explained to Kyle, "That other sword is known as, The Guardian, and can never be replaced. It is a one of a kind katana and so is the tanto, its mate."

It was evident in Kyle's facial expression that he didn't know what Aiko was talking about. "What's the difference between a katana and a tanto?"

Aiko stared at the sword in her hands. "The katana, which you call a samurai sword, weighs about two and a half pounds."

She gripped the handle and slowly withdrew the sword from its scabbard. "It has a single, slender, curved blade with a tsuka, what you call the handle. It is usually between 10 and 11 inches long so it can be used with two hands." Aiko reflected light off the blade into Kyle's eyes. "They've been around since between the 14th and 15th century. In the early 16th century, some katanas were made with shorter blades but then later, near the end of the 16th century, they returned to the original length of about 28 inches."

"And, the tanto?"

"They are usually about 12 inches long but can vary in length. There is also a medium-sized sword that is known as a wakizashi."

"Wow, you really know your stuff."

"Yes," Aiko said, mimicking Kyle. "I know my stuff."

"What makes them so special?"

"Legend has it that there is a set of swords made by a master swordsmith, Masamune, but they were never signed."

"Why not?"

"According to my master, they were made for an ancestor of his, but this great warrior died in battle before the katana's handle could be finished."

"What are they worth?"

"The same as you. Do you have a price? What is your worth? What am I worth?"

Since this was an impossible question for Kyle to answer, he continued with another one, "Why are they important to you, Aiko?"

"Because they are important to my master. It has been a long tradition and a sense of honor to have a set made specifically for someone. And upon death, the swords are buried alongside their owner and taken on his journey in the afterlife."

"I still don't understand. Why is he willing to kill for something that already belongs to him?"

"The tanto which is usually passed on from father to son, was not passed on to my master from his father."

"Why not?"

"I have already told you, honor. He is not an honorable man."

"Then why do you stay with him?"

Aiko did not answer. Instead, she slid the katana back into its scabbard and lowered her eyes. "Are you familiar with the term, *Giri*?

"No."

"It can be translated many ways but in the Japanese culture it can mean the burden of obligation or to avenge one's master's death. It can also mean by saving my life, I no longer belong to Masato, I now have a sense of duty to you and my loyalty is yours."

"Wait a minute. I saved your life because it was my duty."

Instead of feeling the meaning behind his words he had just said to Aiko, Kyle realized his response was without compassion, and he felt only regret, "That didn't come out right. I'm sorry."

Aiko did not have to forgive Kyle, but she did. "Thank you for the gifts. You are a kind man, Kyle Morrell."

The sword gave Aiko rejuvenation to start a whole new set of exercises, this time with the sword. Kyle watched in awe as the mysterious woman before him sliced the sword through the air in a graceful routine. It was as if the sword was an extension of her arm.

"How long did it take you to learn how to do that?"

There was no answer from Aiko as she continued with grace and perfect control of her body's precise movements. Her balance was one with the sword and made her actions look like the lines of poetry.

"Oh, a long time," Kyle mumbled to himself. "Have you ever killed anyone?" Again, there was no response from Aiko, so he answered his own question. "Why no, Kyle, would you like to be the first?"

Aiko dropped to one knee and continued her routine. Beginning to think Aiko was just trying to show off, Kyle blurted out, "Isn't being on one knee a disadvantage?"

The sword stopped in midair, Aiko slipped the sword back into its scabbard and motioned for Kyle to come closer to her. As soon as he was in reach, she slapped him with the end of the scabbard on his inner right thigh and then his left one before he had the chance to understand what was happening.

"Hey!" Kyle said as he jumped back out of reach. "Watch what you're doing."

Aiko again encouraged Kyle to come closer to her. This time, he hesitated. She reversed the sword, held onto the scabbard and offered Kyle the handle. She motioned for him to take it.

As he gripped the handle, Aiko drew the scabbard away. Again, she signaled Kyle to advance. Unsure what to do with it, he tilted his head like a curious puppy. He then reached out and tapped the blade on the end of the scabbard as if to gesture a gentleman's way of announcing "ready to begin." It was too late. Kyle was too close. In the blink of an eye, Aiko whacked him on the back of his hand with the end of the scabbard, knocking the weapon free. Before the sword hit the floor, Aiko reached out and caught it by the handle and placed it into the scabbard.

"You hesitated, Kyle. You had one second to live and you just wasted it."

Aiko offered Kyle the sword again. He accepted it by withdrawing it from the scabbard. He took a step back, then another, to what he thought was out of reach from Aiko. She gestured for him to advance. Kyle didn't move.

"How do I win?" The detective asked.

"What is your life worth?"

Kyle waited for a moment before turning the sword on its side and with two hands, offered it back to Aiko.

She stood up and put the sword back into its protective wooden scabbard.

"A sword at rest can do as much as one drawn, if the one holding it is a master."

"I understand now. My weakness was assuming I had the advantage because you were on one knee."

"Yes, that is true. There is a saying, 'We learn little from victory, much from defeat.'"

Out of the corner of his eye, Kyle saw the laundry basket sitting a few feet away. He went to it and took out a burgundy colored pillowcase. Aiko didn't move as he placed it over her head and spun her around before taking a few steps back. Neither the pillow case nor the body spins seemed to affect Aiko. She continued with her drill exercises as before. Her temporary impairments seemed to emphasize her refined skills. Amazed more than ever at this injured beauty's exhibition, Kyle held his breath. Before he let it out, Aiko tapped him on both shoulders with the sword.

"You heard my breathing," said Kyle. As quietly as possible, he pivoted to the side. Aiko tapped him on the chest.

"The carpet."

This time, Kyle was on his knees, sitting patient and still as the samurai geisha circled around him, never once bumping into him.

"Amaz—," he started to say, when the word was cut off as the scabbard was swiftly and with deadly accuracy placed up under his chin. Aiko slowly drew it across his throat.

The words were barely audible from Kyle's mouth, "So, this is who you are?"

"I am grateful for what I have been taught."

"Living by the sword is not a life."

"According to who, Kyle. You?"

Kyle listened to Aiko's voice for any trace of softness. Hearing none, he continued with his questions. "How long did it take for you to become this cold and calculating?"

"It is how, like the tempered steel in this blade, we are formed."

"What about feelings?"

"I can feel the pillowcase on my head."

Kyle removed the pillowcase from Aiko's head and looked into her dark eyes. "So, do you like the sword I bought you?"

"It is nothing more than a fancy letter opener."

"Oh, really?"

"That is what I said."

The pillowcase was still in Kyle's hand so he put it back on Aiko's head.

She removed the sword from its scabbard and instructed Kyle to step back. With one back-hand wield, she sliced through the top six inches of three thick pieces of bamboo growing in a flower pot on the coffee table. Aiko removed the pillowcase and handed it to Kyle. Noticing her clean sword slice, she commented, "Maybe not, in the hands of a master."

"I guess you can see well enough through that pillowcase, it's like cheesecloth," Kyle commented.

Aiko handed the pillowcase and the sword to Kyle. She stepped back, inviting him to take the challenge. "Not like cheesecloth. Very high thread count."

Kyle looked at the remaining ten inches of the bamboo stock, then pulled the pillowcase over his head and gripped the sword. He visualized the pot of bamboo and took a deep breath. Aiko walked farther and farther away from the living room.

"Aaaaahhhhh," Kyle shouted as he attempted the same maneuver as Aiko. His result was much different than hers. The sword had made contact with the bamboo, but the blade grabbed the stalk of the bamboo and the pot went flying across the room, crashing against the wall upon impact.

Aiko put her hand to her mouth to stifle the small laugh that wanted to escape from her lips.

Still wearing the pillowcase, Kyle's voice was muffled as he asked Aiko, "Can you help me? Can you tell me where Masato has taken Oksana?"

When he finally removed the pillowcase, she was gone.

Chapter 14

Silent prayers filled Oksana's mind like an out-of-control storm. She begged God to rescue her from this nightmare. Earlier, she had been instructed to remove her clothes and put on a white robe. From there she was then told to lay down on a narrow bed with white sheets, her pleas to be saved came faster and stronger. The tears in her eyes were barely contained as she squeezed her eyelids shut as tight as possible. Masato's voice was talking to her and she wished she could put her hands over her ears so she couldn't hear him.

"Oksana, it is time."

Reluctantly, the frightened teenager opened her eyes just as Masato reached out his hand to help her up from the bed. Refusing his assistance, Oksana sat up and then stood up by herself. She followed her captor over to the elevator. Masato took out his swipe card, passed it by the sensor and unlocked the elevator doors. Once inside, Masato hit the button for the second floor. As the doors closed and the elevator headed down, Oksana knew her world was about to change forever. The elevator stopped and so did her hopes of being rescued. The doors opened and Oksana couldn't move, her legs were frozen by the fear of the unknown.

Masato took her hand and assured her, "Not to worry, you will do fine." He led her past a gorgeous blonde woman in her early 20's who watched a bank of monitors. Oksana made every attempt to observe her surroundings, hoping she could find an obvious escape route. The best she could figure out was that the second and third floors of this old warehouse had been converted to one large room. The floor she was on had several rooms that were set up to look like various locations. Masato led Oksana to the far side of the floor where the two walls had come together to form the back of the set. It was completely tiled and constructed to look like the showers in a girl's high school locker room.

A light steam swirled around the shower head area. Oksana glanced around her and gasped at what she saw. Young girls not much older than her, stood naked beneath shower heads, washing each other.

"We are waiting, Oksana," Masato said.

Once again, fear paralyzed Oksana.

Masato leaned in, "You can do this, or you can choose to never be heard from again. I will leave it up to you."

Oksana slowly untied her robe and let it drop to the floor. She gingerly stepped into the shower stall in front of her. As she stood beneath the stream of water from the shower, she stayed facing the wall, hoping the water flowing down around her, along with the steam, would hide her nakedness.

Masato stepped back and studied the movie set around him. The mock shower stalls and locker room were designed to be realistic in appearance. He spared no expense in the little details or the sophisticated camera equipment used to record the pornographic shows.

A wicked smile of approval spread across his face as he watched underage females undress each other in the locker room area. From there, he began his daily rounds of inspection of the other stages. These included a dorm room with a girl on a laptop, web chatting with a client and a secretary sitting at her office desk, unbuttoning her blouse in front of a computer monitor. There was a standard home kitchen with a naked woman, except for an apron, doing dishes at the sink. A man walked up behind her and put his arms around her. Then she saw a convertible with the top down. Behind it was a large curtain of a nighttime city skyline.

A girl was sitting on the lap of a man in the front passenger seat, facing him as they kissed.

Masato made his way over to the monitoring station and started caressing the shoulders of Erica, a younger American version of Aiko. She was a woman he personally designated as his own star pupil. He found her long blonde hair and fair skin quite erotic so he took her off the market for himself.

When Erica spoke to Masato, it was like a cat purring. "The bidding is about to begin."

Masato watched the monitor as an 18-year-old girl modeled a 17th-century vase. "The girl has been with us for almost two years. She just turned 18."

"She will be whatever age we put on the documents at the close of sale. Make her 17."

Erica quickly changed the graphics on the 18th-century vase for sale, to 17th-century.

"It's time. All the participants are ready," Masato boasted. "I say 75, but let's start it at 25."

Erica set the internal clock for five minutes and opened the bid at $25,000. She and Masato watched as the bid quickly jumped to $30,000, to $40,000, $50,000, and then $60,000. Just before the time ran out, Erica commented, "Almost, but not quite."

"Wait for it," Masato said confidently.

With 10 seconds to go the bid reached $100,000.

Masato bragged, "Sold!" He leaned over, kissed Erica on the neck as his hand rubbed her back. He whispered in her ear, "I will never let you go, for any price."

"Easy money," thought Masato as he headed back toward the high school shower set. He noticed Oksana hadn't moved since she first entered the stall.

"Oksana, take that bar of soap in front of you and wash yourself," Masato demanded. "Look up above the showerhead and smile into the camera."

Oksana looked up towards the camera and forced an unwilling smile on her face.

"That's it, you're doing fine. Now turn around and look at us."

She hesitated.

"Do it now, Oksana. I'm not going to ask you again."

Oksana obeyed and turned to face the console area.

One of the men operating a camera in the media control center, zoomed in on Oksana's face, while a man at the controls of the edit bay hit a button displaying the words CLOSE UP.

*****

Oksana's face filled the screen on Masato's laptop that sat open on his desk. He ran his finger over the monitor as if caressing her while he talked on the phone to a potential buyer.

"As you can see by the photo, Mr. Smith, she is a very pretty girl. For the right price, you can have her all to yourself." There was a slight pause before Masato answered the voice at the other end. "Yes, she is a virgin, I checked myself." More silence before Masato replied, "Yes, the bidding starts at midnight and, as usual, cash only."

After the phone call, Masato grabbed a beer while he turned the volume up on his TV. The local news was on and a pretty brunette field reporter was interviewing Captain Morrell.

"Captain Morrell, can you please tell us more about the missing girl from the warehouse shooting?"

"I have no comment at this time," replied Captain Morrell.

"That's right, my Captain," Masato said out loud, "You're—"

The ringing phone on Masato's desk interrupted his remark. "Yes." He listened to the voice at the other end. "Good. Are you sure about the address?" There was silence then Masato ended the conversation with, "Then get it done . . . tonight."

After lighting a cigar, Masato leaned back in his black leather office chair and smiled to himself. He thought about the surprised look on Aiko's exquisite face as he exhaled a ring of smoke from his cigar into the air and watched it fade away.

Chapter 15

Steam rose from the stir-fry pan on the stove as Aiko tossed in pieces of diced chicken that sizzled in peanut oil in the bottom of the wok. It glazed to a light golden brown as she occasionally stirred it with a set of wooden chopsticks. She added an assortment of fresh vegetables, stirring faster as not to overcook them. When the Asian cuisine was ready, she put it on plates with a side of white rice.

Before setting the plates on the kitchen table, Aiko walked over to Kyle, wearing her new jeans and a red t-shirt, and gave him 'that look'. The same look Kyle had seen before, and he hit the remote button that turned off the TV.

As they sat down for dinner, Aiko said, "Thank you for the jeans."

"They look very nice on you." Kyle gave her an appreciative look.

Aiko looked down at her food as she softly replied, "Thank you."

"The other day I saw you sitting on the back porch and you were smiling. What were you thinking about?"

"Memories I don't wish talk about."

Aiko used a fresh pair of wooden chopsticks and Kyle used a fork, shoveling in his food like it was his last meal. He took a bite while mumbling, "Not sharp enough."

Aiko gave Kyle a puzzled look.

"Sorry." After Kyle finished his bite, he said, "You mentioned the katana could have been a little sharper."

"It is okay."

Kyle got up and returned with the katana and set it on the edge of the table. "You said it was nothing more than a fancy letter opener. Well, while you were in the shower, I ran it through the electric knife sharpener at least a dozen times. Now you have a really sharp letter opener."

Aiko found his attempt to make her gift more to her liking, worthy of a story.

"Okay, you want a story. One afternoon, our sensei took a group of us to watch a sword master create a katana. I remember our sensei telling us that when the sword master finished making the sword, he would test the sharpness of the blade by dropping a grain of rice on to its edge, to see if it would cut the piece of rice in half."

"Seriously?"

Aiko didn't answer. Instead, she took a small bite from her plate, her way of playing cat and mouse. Kyle was so caught up in her story; he didn't realize he had almost finished his portion of the stir-fry.

"Did you even taste it?"

"Yes. Thank you, Aiko. It was very good."

"You are welcome. Is this not better than a pizza?"

Kyle put the last forkful of stir-fry in his mouth, giving him a few more seconds before he had to answer the question.

"It depends." Kyle's response was interrupted by a knock at the door. His hands went up in a defensive position as he said, "Hey, I didn't order anything."

Since only a couple of people knew that Kyle and Aiko were staying on the houseboat, wariness swept over their faces.

"Go to the back bedroom and shut the door, Aiko," Kyle urged.

Instead, while Kyle looked through the peephole in the door, Aiko walked to the corner of the living room with her katana.

"It's okay, it's Officer Pena," Kyle said. He opened the door to let the officer in and set his weapon down on the table near the door.

As Pena made his way in, Kyle shut the door and locked the deadbolt.

"Hey, Pena, how's it going?"

"Not bad, Morrell. How's the babysitting job going? You two getting along okay?" Pena, his back to Kyle, took a good look at Aiko while he spoke to Kyle.

Kyle noticed the way Pena was focusing his attention on Aiko and it gave him an uneasy feeling.

"Any word on Masato's location?"

"No, not yet," replied Pena.

Kyle lightly slapped Pena on the shoulder in an attempt to get him to turn around and face him. As Pena obliged, Kyle quickly shot a glance at Aiko and understood by the way she was shaking her head, something wasn't right. Kyle continued to engage Pena in conversation. "We were just getting ready to sit down and eat. Would you like to join us? There's plenty."

"No, I'm here for another reason." Pena's handgun was suddenly pointed at Kyle. He motioned for him to move over by Aiko.

"Here, put these on." Pena tossed a pair of handcuffs to Kyle. "Your right hand, Kyle, to her left."

Kyle slowly put the cuffs on his right hand. "Why are you doing this, Pena?"

"None of your business why I'm doing this, Morrell," Pena said irritably. "Aiko, your left hand, please."

The astute woman glared at Pena, sized him up and refused to comply. Pena pointed the gun at her. When Aiko still refused, he pointed it at Kyle.

Slowly Aiko's left hand came out from behind her back, her sword firmly in her grasp.

"Well, well, well. Didn't anyone ever tell you not to bring a knife to a gunfight?" Pena chuckled at the tired cliché.

Aiko dropped the sword at her side, between her and Kyle, with the handle pointed toward Pena. Kyle attached the other half of the handcuffs to Aiko's left wrist.

"Clearly you have the upper hand, Pena. What do you want?"

The purchased cop took out a silencer and spun it firmly onto the end of his weapon.

"Morrell, you might want to take a moment to say adios to your muchacha."

Kyle looked into Aiko's eyes. "Whatever you do, don't get on your knees for this guy."

"Hey, Morrell, aren't you even going to ask who sent me to kill you and your little friend here?"

Before Kyle could respond, Pena quipped, "Your father sent me."

"My father?" A look of shock swept over Kyle's face.

"No, her father," replied Pena.

From an inner jacket pocket, Pena withdrew an envelope and tossed it to Kyle. "This is a copy of the lab results from Aiko's rape kit. It proves not only is Masato Aiko's master, he is also her biological father."

Fury overtook any fear Aiko was feeling. She managed to hold back a flood of tears, but one small drop escaped and slid down her cheek.

"You bastard!" Kyle shouted.

Aiko looked at Kyle. "You knew?" She could no longer contain the emotional riptide inside of her. Quiet sobs erupted and she dropped to her knees. The pull from the handcuffs caused Kyle to drop to one knee next to Aiko.

A malicious sneer appeared on Pena's face. He seemed to enjoy the dramatic scene being played out before him. "You didn't tell her, Morrell? Shame on you."

Kyle leaned in toward the dirty cop. "She didn't need to know."

Pena pointed his gun at Aiko's head. Kyle started to rise as if to go after Pena but then thought better of it.

"Come on, you really think you can jump me before I pull this trigger and take her out?"

As the two men taunted each other eye to eye, Aiko gripped the scabbard with her left hand near the hilt.

"So, who's going to go first?" Pena stepped back so he wouldn't get blood on his shirt from the blowback. His gun still pointed at Aiko's head, "You, Aiko?"

Pena then turned his gun on Kyle and pointed at his head. "Or you?"

In the time it took for Pena to point the gun at Kyle, Aiko reached across her body with her right hand, gripped the handle of her katana and in one flawless, fluid, upward motion, drew the sword and sliced off Pena's hand. It dropped to the floor, the gun still in its grip. Blood squirted from his wrist, sprayed across Aiko's face and down her neck.

Before Pena could make a sound, Aiko pivoted on her knees and sent the blade upward under Pena's rib cage.

The katana passed through his lung, then into his heart, killing him instantly. She withdrew the blade as quickly as it went in and watched Pena fall to the floor with a dead drop thud.

"Are you alright?" Kyle asked.

Aiko didn't reply. Instead, she held one finger to her mouth and whispered, "We need to go, now."

Making an about-face, Aiko slipped the katana under the couch just before Kyle took her by the hand and led her out the sliding glass door to the patio deck. As Kyle closed the sliding door behind them, he could hear the front door being kicked in. Out of the corner of his eye, he saw another cop enter the houseboat.

Chapter 16

Both Aiko and Kyle let out a small gasp as they slid from the deck of the houseboat into the dark, frigid waters of the Columbia River. They each took a deep breath and slipped beneath the water's edge. They swam over to the next houseboat, the distance no wider than one could store a small boat, and came up in the shadows. Kyle made a motion with his hand indicating Aiko should swim under the pontoon and come up under the houseboat's floating deck. Coming up in a small pocket under the deck, they were able to see the back porch of Kyle's place through a narrow gap in the pontoons. They watched as the sliding glass door opened and the cop stepped out on the deck.

It was nothing more than a cursory look around by the cop before he went back inside. Still handcuffed together, Kyle and Aiko swam from one houseboat to another until they were a decent distance from Kyle's place.

"Did you know Masato was my father?" Aiko stared hard at Kyle.

"I found out the same time you did."

"You know what else we found out?"

Kyle's expression was one of confusion.

"We both have been betrayed by our fathers. Your father was the only person who knew where we were."

Long seconds passed before Kyle responded, "This cold water isn't doing us any good. We need to find someplace to get you cleaned up and warm as soon as possible."

"Where do you suggest we go?"

"I have an idea. Follow me."

Aiko raised her left hand out of the water pulling up Kyle's right hand, reminding him they were still handcuffed together. Her expression said clearly, "Like I have a choice."

After an awkward swim, down to the end of the row of houseboats, Kyle helped Aiko up onto the floating dock. The handcuffs made a soft rattling sound when Aiko clutched Kyle's hands and helped him out of the murky water. They stopped by a houseboat with no lights on.

"One of these has to be a vacation home," Kyle said as he peered through the front door window. "Looks like this one's empty."

"How do you know for sure?" Aiko's teeth were chattering.

Kyle pointed to a sign near the door that read Davenport Real Estate.

"This one has a lockbox just like ours, but I don't know the combination to this one."

Kyle knocked on the door. After a second knock and no obvious noise coming from within, he said, "I hope Alicia will forgive me for this. I already owe her a new door." He picked up the doormat and placed it over the corner pane of glass closest to the deadbolt, throwing his elbow into the mat, smashing out the glass. Kyle reached inside and turned the lock.

A few tiny night lights throughout the unit gave the couple enough illumination to maneuver around safely without turning on any main lights. Kyle noticed Aiko shaking, so he found the thermostat and turned it up.

"Let's see if we can find an owner's closet." Kyle words shuddered as his own body shivered from the lack of core body heat.

"What is that?"

"Owners will sometimes have a special closet that they keep locked with their own belongings in it. That way they don't need to bring everything they need each time they come for a visit. We're going to need a way to get through the lock once we find it."

Kyle took Aiko by the hand into the kitchen.

He checked the refrigerator, noticed a couple of bottles of water and a couple cans of Coke. He handed Aiko a bottle of water and helped himself to a Coke. After satisfying his thirst, he searched kitchen drawers until he found a butter knife and a meat tenderizing mallet. Once again, he held onto Aiko's hand as they wandered the residence.

He found a locked hall closet. Kyle rattled the door handle. "This must be it."

Using the knife and mallet, Kyle popped the pins out of the door hinges and then lifted the door off, setting it against the wall. He turned on the hall light revealing a healthy selection of clothing, towels, toiletries and canned foods. After choosing a variety of items from all the categories, the door was put back in place and the light was turned off. They set their things in the master bedroom then went into the bathroom.

"You're freezing, Aiko. We need to get you warmed up."

Aiko tensed and studied Kyle's facial features for signs of his intentions. Observing only a weariness and physical discomfort, she relaxed and allowed him to guide her into the bathroom. He turned on the shower and let the water to run until it created a soft warm mist that filled the bathroom.

"After all we have been through, we can trust each other, right?" Kyle asked.

Aiko nodded.

Kyle reached into his pocket and removed his set of keys, one of which was a handcuff key. He unlocked the cuffs and attached them to the curtain rod. Aiko looked at Kyle with the possibility that she might be able to trust him after all. She felt the tiniest crack starting to invade the wall she constructed around her heart.

After removing her wet shirt, and tossing it on the floor, Aiko announced, "I trust you, Kyle."

The bandages that covered Aiko's bullet wounds were dirty and loose to the point of falling off. Kyle slowly removed the bandage from her lower left side where the bullet had gone through and through at the fleshy part of her waist, just above her hip. He then reached around her waist and felt for the other bandage and pulled it off. The stitches were coated with dried blood and dirt from the river.

Aiko's bra covered the bandage along the left side of her ribcage. She reached back and unhooked it and let it fall to the floor. Kyle did his best to maintain eye contact with her as she lifted her arm enough for him to carefully remove the dirty bandage.

"Step into the shower, Aiko."

She removed her jeans and entered the shower. Kyle reached over and grabbed the can of Coke off the bathroom counter.

Confusion materialized on Aiko's face, "What are you going to do with that?"

Kyle poured the Coke over the dirty stitches.

"The fizz of carbon dioxide will work like a peroxide and help clean out your stitches."

"You are a man of many resources."

"It's the least I can do," Kyle said, a sheepish grin spreading across his face. Again, Aiko raised her arm as he poured Coke over the small set of stitches that lined her ribs.

"What do you mean?"

"Let's just leave it at that, shall we?"

Aiko stepped back and put her head under the spray of the warm shower as Kyle unbuttoned his white dress shirt and tossed it into the heap of wet clothes on the floor. A puddle formed in the middle of the bathroom floor, its size doubling when Kyle's jeans were added to the pile.

As Kyle stepped into the shower, Aiko faced away from him, making her white tiger tattoo the center of his vision. Never had he seen anything so captivating. Kyle could only mutter one word. "Stunning."

Not wanting to give Aiko the wrong idea, he added, "The tattoo I mean."

Aiko did not let him see the slight smile that briefly crossed her face. Putting shampoo in his hands, Kyle began to gently massage it through Aiko's ebony colored hair. The gesture was so tender and unexpected, she found it hard to believe it was the hands of a man performing the act.

After rinsing, she turned around and held out her hands. Kyle grabbed the shampoo and squeezed a shot into them.

"Turn around, please," Aiko said. She reached up to wash his hair but found it difficult. "You are too tall," she stated.

Kyle knelt down, his back to her. "That's better," she said. She removed the shower wand from its holder to rinse Kyle's hair. "Do you trust me?" Aiko asked.

"Yes."

"I need to go after the girl, and I need to do it alone."

"No."

"It is about honor and I cannot risk you getting killed over my responsibilities."

"You are now my responsibility, Aiko, and I wouldn't be doing my job if I let you go and get yourself killed on my watch."

Aiko turned around and hung up the shower wand.

"I am sorry if I am such a burden to you."

"I don't ever want you to think that, Aiko."

Kyle stood and used the small bar of hotel soap to wash Aiko's back and around her wounds. He softly kissed her shoulder. She displayed no reaction at his attempt of expressing some sensitivity and tenderness. In fact, nothing in her actions or words allowed him to read her emotions at all. As he reached down to wash her backside wound, he dropped to one knee. Once the wound was clean, he kissed her near the stitches as if to say, "There, all better now."

Aiko showed no response to this gesture either. Slowly she turned around. Kyle's lathered hands washed around the wound on the front side at her waist. He kissed her again near the wound. No reaction. He continued to kiss Aiko below her belly button and just above her panty line, his hands running up the back of her thighs. This time, he felt her body quiver from his touch. Kyle stood and faced Aiko.

The defensiveness in Aiko's liquid brown eyes seemed less prominent and without thinking, Kyle's fingertips touched her cheek.

"I'm going to hell for this," Aiko whispered.

"I'm going to hell with you," Kyle replied.

Pulling her close to his body, Kyle caressed her shoulder and back. As his hands moved further south, she stopped him. Feeling her body tense, Kyle stepped back, panic in his eyes as he looked into hers. "What's wrong, did I hurt you?"

"No, I'm afraid I will not be able to feel what you want me to feel."

Unsure of what to do next, Kyle tried to hold Aiko, but it felt awkward because he didn't know exactly where to place his hands.

After a few moments Aiko said, "We still have a problem." She arched her eyebrows, a look indicating she wanted Kyle to do something. "The towels were left on the bed."

"I'll be right back," said Kyle.

With only a towel around his waist, he put his and Aiko's washed clothing into the dryer. A small item of clothing had clung to the inside of the washer. When he pulled away and unraveled it, he realized it was Aiko's panties. A grin radiated across his face.

Returning to the bedroom, Kyle saw Aiko asleep in the bed, still in her towel. In the ambient light, he sat in the chair near the bed and watched her sleep.

He thought about what he had read in a book called Pictures of the Floating World. It was about the world of carnal desires. It said that geisha meant a person of the arts. The whole idea of being one was about perfection, drawing men in like a moth to a flame.

Kyle's heart was torn. What he felt for Aiko was like a wonderful mystery yet to unfold. She was like the moon, always at a distance; and for now, only able to see one side of her. In contrast, he felt that his feet were firmly planted on the earth. Right now, more than anything, he wanted to wake her, touch her skin and kiss her. Instead, he let her dream.

Chapter 17

The glow of the burning embers increased as Aiko watched the master swordsmith prepare the furnace for a samurai sword that would be created from a raw steel called *tamahage,* which is made from iron, sand, carbon, and charcoal. The sound of the bellows pumping oxygen to the hot coals and bringing the embers to life was still a strong memory for Aiko. She was twelve years old when the sensei brought her to observe the sword master, known as a Kaji, create the samurai sword. As the Kaji shoved the rod of tempered steel into the hot coals, forging the sword, Aiko felt the heat released as he rhythmically began adding more oxygen to the coals. The glow from the coals turned bright orange, to yellow, to white as the Kaji softened the steel enough to fold it. He quickly moved the steel rod from the 800-degree furnace to the anvil. He hammered it flat, then returned it to the fire to heat it once again. From there it went to the anvil to be folded and flattened even more.

Aiko's sensei told her that he must do this over and over, reheating and pounding it out, again and again, creating layer upon layer, forming the body of the katana's blade.

A dozen or more folds would create over 5000 layers per one centimeter of steel.

The heat did not bother Aiko. She was fascinated by it and stepped closer to the coals to get a better look as the Kaji struck the molten steel. Sparks flew like fireworks in every direction. One landed on the inside of Aiko's left arm and she quickly brushed it off. She joined her classmates and watched as the sword master began to split the top of the steel rod.

"What is he doing now, sensei?" Aiko asked.

"Creating a U-shaped channel where he will hammer in another piece of low carbon steel, making it fit very snug and then he will forge the two metals together."

Later, one of the other students asked, "What is a painting?"

"The swordsmith paints a mixture of clay with charcoal on the blade, creating thin layers on the cutting-edge and thicker amounts to the back, before quenching it in the water. This way the steel will take on two completely different properties. Giving the blade the hard-cutting edge it requires, and a suppler back. Because of the different speeds in which the two halves of the steel are cooled, the forming of the steel takes on the curved edge of the samurai sword.

The curve design was created to make it easier for the samurai to slice. Before, one would have to strike and then pull to create penetration. With the curved blade, the penetration happens on impact allowing the slice to go deeper with less effort."

The students gathered around another Kaji and watched as he polished a sword. This action revealed the hamon, a wavy design that was etched into the blade from when the clay and charcoal were painted on. The designs were unique to each sword and acted like a signature, with each swordsmith adding his own bit of style and flair. The Kaji let a few of the students choose from a basket of colored threads until they picked the one he already had in mind to make the handle. Later that evening, they sat around a campfire and watched as he added the hilt and wrapped the threads around the handle, making it complete.

A cool breeze sent a chill up Aiko's back. The flames from the fire mesmerized her as they reflected off the side of the blade. She closed her eyes tightly. When she opened them, the dream was gone and Kyle was sitting across from her.

"Are you okay?"

"I will be. I am still cold."

Kyle circled to his side of the bed, let his towel fall to the floor, and climbed into bed. As Aiko lay on her side, Kyle cautiously slipped up behind her. He pulled the covers tightly over both of them then wrapped his arms around her.

"Is this okay?"

"Yes. Are you going to have your way with me now?"

"I—"

"You deserve me. You saved my life. I can belong to you now."

"Aiko, you don't belong to anyone anymore. Whatever you desire to do, it will be your choice."

They had no idea how much time had passed, but without warning, Aiko turned to face Kyle. The heat generated from the blankets and their bodies had developed to the point Aiko could no longer just lie there. She pushed Kyle on his back then positioned herself on top of him. He was about to say something when she put her finger to his lips. Surprised by the sudden display of affection, Kyle laid perfectly still as Aiko kissed his lips, first delicately, then with a storm-like force. The scent of strawberry shampoo and her soft skin slammed into Kyle's senses, sending his body into the highest gear of desire.

Feeling his physical reaction to her touch, Aiko reached down and guided Kyle's manhood into her. They continued to kiss as his hands ran over the towel she wore. He could feel the form of her strong, lithe body. Kyle sat up and Aiko wrapped her legs around his waist. The towel slipped off her body and he pulled her close, feeling the softness of her breasts against his chest. He kissed her on the neck and the taste of her skin was warm and luscious, a mixture of her body's natural sweet passion and saltiness. As his strong hands slid down the length of her back, he pulled her in tighter. Their kisses fed an emotional hunger for both of them. Aiko never believed tenderness like this would have been possible for her. Waves of ecstasy traveled through her entire body as they climaxed together. As she collapsed, she wept.

"Are you all right?"

Aiko tried to catch her breath while mumbling something in her native Japanese.

"Translation?"

"I will be. I have never felt this way before."

"How's that?"

"In control."

"I have to tell you something." Kyle's eyes couldn't hide his regret. "I shot you first."

Aiko tried to say something, but he put his finger gently over her lips. "And for that, I am truly sorry. It was a ricochet."

Aiko pulled his hand away from her lips and placed it over the wound on her rib.

"So, this is from you?" She then lowered his hand to the wound on the side of her waist.

"This is from the man who tried to kill me."

"Let me check your other stitches."

Aiko rolled over. Kyle ran his fingertips gently around the stitches along the side of her waist, then lightly upward along her spine.

"How long did it take them to do this?"

"It took two artists almost a week."

"Why this design?"

"It is what my master wanted."

"And you knew he was your father?"

"I knew him as the man who took me away from that orphanage and trained me to be a samurai and a geisha. He raised me. He was my master. I never knew he was my father."

"What happened to your mother?"

"I do not know. I assumed both of my parents died or why would I have been in such a place?"

"Now that you know, what are you going to do?"

"I have to save Oksana, or she will end up like me, damaged."

"You are not damaged, Aiko. There is so much about you that is right, that I want to get to know. There is so much I want to share with you, if you will let me."

"You are a kind man, Kyle Morrell." She kissed him gently.

"You know your father wants you dead, Aiko."

"He won't kill me. I have information he needs."

"It sure looked like he was trying to kill you in the hospital," Kyle retorted, hoping Aiko understood his frustration was not with her. "What information?"

"I am the only one who knows where the tanto is hidden."

"How is it that you know and Masato doesn't? And why not give it to him? Maybe he would leave you alone."

"That is not his way, Kyle. I defied him; therefore, I embarrassed him in front of many important people connected with his organization. Once he has the tanto, he will try to kill me."

Kyle bristled and wrapped Aiko in his arms. "He will never touch you again."

"The tanto is important, but not as important as freeing the young girls held captive by Masato." Aiko slipped away from Kyle's arms to study his face. "I have a way we can rescue the girls and get the tanto."

Running his hand over the two-day stubble on his face, Kyle didn't want to hear Aiko's plan. He wanted to take her to the other side of the world, where no one could hurt her again.

Softly, Kyle asked, "What did you have in mind?"

"The tunnels."

"Tunnels? What tunnels?"

"There are a series of tunnels known as The Shanghai Tunnels that run under the city. Masato has bought properties that sit over one of these tunnels and uses it to move the girls without being seen."

"Won't the tunnel be guarded by Masato's men?" Kyle asked.

Aiko made her point. "They are watching for the girls who are trying to get out, not for those trying to get in."

Chapter 18

Exhaustion kept Kyle in a deep sleep. It was only when morning sunshine hit his eyes and he tried to turn away from it, did he finally wake up. Immediately he realized his right hand was handcuffed to the headboard and Aiko was no longer lying next to him.

"Damn," Kyle muttered as he glanced around. His eyes finally rested on a folded note on the nightstand, which he picked up. The handcuff key slid out of the note and Kyle managed to grab it before it dropped to the floor. Only two words were scribbled on the note. THANK YOU.
He doubted Aiko was still in the houseboat, but Kyle searched anyway. His final stop was the laundry room where he found his clothes neatly folded on the dryer. That is, everything but his white dress shirt; it was missing.

Frustrated that Aiko didn't want his help to rescue Oksana, Kyle debated on what his next move would be, go after Masato or go after Aiko. After returning unused items back to the closet, Kyle put the bed sheets in the washing machine and turned it on.

In a short letter to Alicia, he apologized for using the place without permission, thanked her and left a damp one-hundred-dollar bill with the note.

The morning air chilled Kyle's bare chest as he made his way down the dock to his houseboat. Seeing no one around, he entered and noticed Officer Pena's body gone. He checked under the couch and saw the katana he gave to Aiko was gone as well. Kyle grabbed another shirt and put it on as he walked through the unit assessing the damage. Feeling restless and with some apprehension, he made a phone call.

"Hey Dad, it's me. I need you to come pick me up at the houseboat."

"Are you okay, son?"

"Officer Pena and someone I didn't recognize tried to kill us last night."

"What are you talking about? What about Aiko. Is she okay?"

"She's gone. Just come and get me. I think I know where she's headed. I'm worried she's going after Masato."

"Does she have a gun?"

"No, she has a katana."

*****

It was after ten and the night air temperature had dropped another few degrees. Aiko, standing in the shadow of a receded doorway, was wearing her red t-shirt tucked into her blue jeans and Kyle's white dress shirt. The sleeves were rolled up to just below the elbows and the long front shirttails had been tied into a knot at her waist.

Across the street, The Pearl Night Club boasted a neon entrance designed to appeal to the indiscriminating senses of young adults. From within the club's deep interior, fast-tempo music escaped through the front door, its finger pulling immature and inexperienced girls, like Anna, into its grasp.

Igor, a well-dressed bouncer, scrutinized Anna before he scanned her ID a second time. He could tell the ID was a fake but she fit what the nightclub called for: young with a bit of charm, pretty with a childlike innocence, from out of town, a naiveté about her and of course . . . alone.

"Have a good time, Anna," he said. As she entered the club, he punched a code into his hand-held scanner.

Aiko continued to watch as mini-groups of young women giggled and flirted with the good-looking bouncer.

His charm drew them in like moths to the flame. Her arms were crossed and she tried to control the sick gut feeling of what these girls could be in for, trying instead to stay focused on her mission. She gripped the katana with one hand, pinned it to her side and hid it along her silhouette so as not to cause undue attention.

*****

Anna was unaware she was being watched as she navigated her way past the mahogany covered antique bar. The surveillance camera above the end of the bar followed her as she approached an even bigger bouncer. At the end of the bar was Arlo, well over six feet tall and pushing three hundred pounds.

Anna raised herself up onto her toes to read his name tag. "Arlo," she said with a sweet smile in her voice. "Can you tell me which way to the lady's room?"

He pointed past the other end of the bar.

Anna smiled, "Thank you, kind sir," and headed on her way.

Standing behind Arlo was Ben, one of the club's managers. He was talking to a fresh-off-the-bus girl from Kentucky.

"How do you pronounce your name?"

"It's like Alex but with a 'ks.' Like with a little kiss on the end."

"I notice you don't have any references on your resume."

"Not to worry, I can do the job. I was a waitress at the local café where I used to live. I just don't know anybody here who can give me a reference." Aleks' eyes observed everything around her, except the sinister intentions in Ben's dark eyes.

"You don't know anyone around here?"

"No. I mean yes. The motel where I'm staying, I kinda know the front desk person that works days."

"Wait right here, Aleks with a 'ks', while I go and check the schedule." Ben nodded to a bartender as he headed to an office hidden behind the bar.

Aleks' body reacted to the rhythm of the music, she closed her eyes and whispered a "Thank you for the job" to God.

The bartender made his way to Aleks' end of the bar.

"What can I get ya?"

"I already got it — a job, working here."

The bartender offered his hand. "I'm Peter."

"I'm Aleks."

Peter noticed a small tattoo just above her left breast of a broken heart. "I see you had your heart broken."

"It's more like the other way around. I'm the heartbreaker."

"Where you from, Aleks the heartbreaker?"

"Kentucky."

"Hey, I know a friend of yours."

"Who's that?"

Peter reached down, grabbed a bottle of Jim Beam and poured each of them a shot.

Aleks replied warmly, "Ah, yes, that friend."

As Peter stowed away the bottle of Jim Beam, he hit a button under the bar and the lights began to strobe wildly. People on the dance floor screamed in delight. Peter and Aleks grabbed their shots, saluted, and as Aleks slammed back her shot, Peter tripped a second button under the bar. One second, Aleks was there, and then she was gone. The sad thing was nobody noticed that the young beauty from Kentucky, had disappeared.

*****

When the floor she was standing on suddenly opened up and dropped her with a hard thud onto a mattress, Aleks was too shocked to react with a scream.

Before she could take in what had happened, a bright light was shoved in her face. The pain of a stun gun shot through her body, immediately subduing her. She was quickly dragged off the stack of mattresses by the man with the stun gun while a second man reset the trap door. He then helped to lift the young girl's body up onto the bigger man's shoulders. Aleks was as silent as the tunnel her captors traveled in.

*****

Watching the boats travel up and down the Willamette River had become tedious, so Kyle and Captain Morrell watched the bouncing lights reflecting on the water of the river. An occasional owner walked by with his or her dog and, at one point, a couple argued while riding their bikes, almost swerving into the side of their car.

Sitting in the passenger seat, Kyle contemplated the situation he had been roped into when he first laid eyes on Aiko. In less than a week, she had changed his life. All of a sudden, he felt he was out of his league. The mysterious Japanese woman had doubted him, trusted him, loved him and now left him. Being away from her made him feel the same way as being in her arms the night before, helpless. Aiko had disappeared by choice, and the fate of Oksana was still unknown.

Kyle's thoughts were interrupted by his dad's voice. "Are you sure she's going to show?"

"No, but for now it's all I have to go on," replied Kyle.

"Has she told you anything useful?"

"Like what, Dad?"

"Anything about Masato's dealings or where the hell he hides out. Nobody in law enforcement has been able to pick up a trace of him since the hospital incident." Captain Morrell reached over the steering wheel to the dash and retrieved a half cup of lukewarm coffee.

Kyle stared at his father with a look that was undecipherable to the old man.

Morrell noticed Kyle's gaze. "What?"

"Aiko said Masato has something on you. Is it true?"

Captain Morrell didn't answer. Instead, he dumped the last of his coffee out the window and tossed the cup in the back seat.

"Dad, is it true? Does Masato have something on you?"

A few more uncomfortable moments passed before Morrell spoke, his voice low and tight. "Kyle, it was a long time ago."

"What does he have on you? Does it have anything to do with Mom's death?"

A distressed look registered on Morrell's face. "Why would you say that? What did Aiko say to you?"

"It wasn't Aiko who said something, it was Steven. He said you were there when she was killed."

Morrell rubbed his large hands over his face and through his hair. He looked at Kyle with the saddest eyes his son had ever seen.

"No, I wasn't there, son. I was too late."

Chapter 19

Sweat from Lydia Morrell's forehead rolled down her face and into her frightened hazel eyes. The salty drops irritated and distorted her vision, but it was impossible for her to wipe them away. Her hands were tied and resting on her lap, forced to stay in that position because her arms were duct-taped to her side. Her entire torso was taped to the driver's seat of the car. Her mouth was gagged and her head was duct-taped to the headrest.

Panic set in as Lydia's mind began to clear from being drugged. She knew exactly who had done this to her. But why after all these years of loyalty, why was she now being punished?

In her mind, she was certain she had done what he had instructed for her life to be spared. Marry the policeman, have his children and supply information so he could continue to have the leverage he needed to control the captain.

Inside the hot car, Lydia fervently prayed. She prayed for her husband, her two boys and herself. Trying to be brave was beyond difficult as she stared at the car's steering wheel. The airbag had been removed and the igniter for the airbag had a 12-gauge shotgun shell jammed into it, pointed directly at Lydia's face.

Across the top of the steering wheel, was a red steering wheel security bar that locked the wheel in place so that if the car began to roll, it could only go straight downhill. Beyond the steering wheel, fifty yards down the embankment from where she was parked, was a cement retaining wall.

Unknown to Lydia, a one-gallon plastic bottle of pool acid sat on the vehicle's bumper. A small hole had been punctured in it, allowing a small leak to drip on the rope, which was tied to the car. The rope's deterioration was increased by the hot sun baking the acid through the rope.

Lydia could see the car was in neutral and wondered why it wasn't moving. Then, in the rearview mirror, she saw something, a rope tracing back up the hill that was tied to a tree. She realized then the rope was her lifeline and something else caught her eye in the mirror, a man by the tree. What was he doing? She knew the answer before she could finish her thought. He was there to make sure no one rescued her.

*****

The anger in Kyle's blue eyes dug into Captain Morrell's soul as his dad continued to explain how and why Steven and Kyle's mother died.

"Masato had me. I was told if I looked away

once in a while and let him run his export business without interference, we wouldn't have a problem. Then one day this rookie jumped the gun on a raid and Masato lost some of his girls." Morrell's voice dropped and became barely a whisper. "That rookie was you, Kyle. You were so eager to prove yourself that you couldn't wait for the signal. The plan was—"

Kyle interrupted his father, "What plan? And what did all this have to do with Mom?" Frustration and confusion were evident in Kyle's questions.

"One day at work, I got a call. I thought it was your mom calling to say she had made it home with Steven after school, but it was Masato. He said I had a choice to make, Steven or your mother."

Kyle tried to reach back and bring forward those memories of that day when his mother didn't come home. He remembered that Steven was 12 years old at the time. According to the police report, he was playing in the front yard when a well-dressed, dark-skinned man approached him. The police report said the man had tied Steven up and put duct-tape on his mouth and a note in his pocket.

It was so hot where the man had put Steven

that the young boy had passed out. Steven couldn't recall anything else about that day.

Morrell ignored the distant look in Kyle's eyes and continued with his account of what happened. "Masato had it set up where I only had time to save Steven or your mother. I tried Kyle, you've got to believe me. I tried to save them both. I went to Steven first. Your mother wanted it that way. As it turned out, Steven was tied up in your tree house in the backyard. It scared me to death. He was passed out, suffering from heat stroke. We got him in the house and into a tub of cold water with what ice we had. It wasn't until later on, we noticed your brother had suffered some memory loss from the events of that day. I found the note in his pocket from Masato. That's when you arrived and I had you stay with him while I went to save your mother."

*****

Lydia wasn't sure how much time she had left before her car would be released from the tree it was tied to. She knew when it did, it would roll downhill and hit head-on into the stone retaining wall at the bottom of the hill. Just as Lydia had begun to accept her fate, she heard in the distance, a siren.

Tears washed the sweat from her eyes as the prospect of rescue raced toward her.

Slowly, the pool acid burned through the rope, pulling it apart a strand at a time. It quickly weakened the strength it had to hold the car back. The car jolted and Lydia frantically stomped on the brakes, but the pedal went straight to the floor. No brakes. The car lurched again, another strand gone. In the mirror, she saw the man walk away as the sirens got closer. She knew what the man knew, there wasn't much time left. Then the sirens stopped. The squad car couldn't get any closer.

The duct-tape was so tight around Lydia she felt her heart would burst out of her chest. Glancing one last time in the rearview mirror, she saw her husband come over the top of the hill. She could hear him call her name as he ran down the hill in her direction. The car lurched one last time as the rope snapped and the car began to roll. Lydia was so numb with fear she couldn't feel that she had wet herself. The closer her husband seemed to get, the faster the car sped toward the retaining wall.

"Lydia, Lydia!" She could hear the desperation in her husband's voice. Eyes tightly closed, Lydia visualized her family one last time.

Her unconditional love for them had started a fresh waterfall of tears.

Captain Morrell's world ended when he heard the car hit the wall, followed by a shotgun blast. His legs were no longer a part of him and he collapsed. The sound of the shotgun blast playing over and over as it echoed along the riverfront. Then silence. The stillness that followed it, worse than the horrible sound that preceded it. His heart was beating, but he no longer felt alive. After a long period of time, he found the strength to stand.

The smell of fresh gunpowder was intense as he approached the driver's side of the car. His feet moved like he was walking in blocks of cement. His attention was drawn first to the steering wheel locked in place and then the empty shotgun shell where the airbag should have been. But it was when he saw the monstrosity of one man's wrath that caused his whole world to disappear. He dropped to his knees and with what breath he had left he cried, "I'm sorry, I'm so sorry, Lydia."

*****

Kyle sat perfectly still, his brain searching for parts of the past. His mouth was dry and his tongue felt swollen. He looked over at his dad and noticed the corners of his eyes were moist.

"That's why I don't remember a funeral for Mom."

"I was trying to protect you."

"Why? So you can go on pretending to be the man I thought you were? Steven was right, you got Mom killed."

Morrell's sadness was immediately replaced by anger. "And your actions got your brother killed."

"You weren't there, Dad. When have you ever been there for us? It was always the job with you."

Kyle got out of the car and slammed the door shut.

Morrell exited the vehicle too and asked, "What are you doing?"

"My job!" Kyle started to walk away. "I'm going to get Oksana and reunite her with her father."

"Kyle, wait." Morrell grabbed his son's arm. "Steven was given that assignment because he was expected to fail."

"What?"

"It wasn't supposed to happen the way it did. We made a deal, no one was supposed to get hurt. It was Pankov's way to get the girl to Masato and a way to get us out from under them."

Kyle pulled his arm from his dad's grip. "This was all a deal?"

"It was a legitimate way I could make him a detective because we needed a new face. So what if he failed his first assignment? Others have. And it was going along just fine until he called you in for help."

"Just fine?" Kyle hissed. "So Pankov's shooter taking out the girl's mother was all part of the plan? And you wonder why I don't believe you when you say you had nothing to do with what happened to Mom."

Morrell's voice became louder. "I told you, I wasn't there in time."

"And what about Steven?"

"He would have never been killed if he hadn't called you—"

"Don't you put that one on me." Kyle jabbed his index finger into his dad's chest. "You were the one who made the deal. You were the one who got all this going in the first place. And you know what? Mom is on you too. It wasn't Pankov's men who killed her, it was you."

Morrell shouted at his son as he watched him walk away, "Your mother was the best part of me!"

Kyle turned around and walked back to his father. He hit him with a strong right cross to the face, knocking him to the ground. Holding back the rest of his pent-up anger he said, "Don't."

"You don't understand, your mother was the one who told me to go after Steven first."

Kyle glared at his father. Morrell continued, "When they took Steven, they put your mother on the phone, she knew there was a chance I may not have enough time to save her and Steven." He paused, "She was the one who told me where he was and that there would be a note for me, telling me of her location."

"You still don't get it, Dad. Your looking away all those years is what caused her death."

"And you think by going to The Pearl or knocking on Masato's door, he's just going to hand over the girl and his whore?"

Without a second glance, Kyle turned and walked away, his dad still lying on the ground. Morrell got up and dusted himself off. He looked down and saw his badge on the ground and assumed it came off during the scuffle with his son. He yelled to Kyle as he saw him walk away for what could be the last time.

"You think you got what it takes to confront Masato and risk your life for some Asian woman you don't even know? Do ya?" As Morrell wiped a small amount of blood off his mouth, he said softly, "I hope so, son."

Chapter 20

The human traffic had slowed down at the entrance of The Pearl nightclub. Known as the jewel of Masato's investments, it was located in the area of downtown Portland called the Pearl District. Masato used the club to show off his goods, as well as survey potential money-makers. The district was formerly wall-to-wall warehouses, light industry, and railroad yards. More recently, it was noted for its art galleries, high-end businesses, micro-breweries, and warehouse-to-loft conversions. Ever since the late '90s, Masato exploited his advantage of owning the three properties that lined up over one vein of the Shanghai Tunnels.

Aiko continued to observe the crowds from across the street, ignoring the increased coolness of the night air. Just when she thought she had misjudged her timing, familiar figures exited the nightclub. A taxi pulled up next to the group and Aiko watched as Oksana was helped into the cab by Hitoshi, Masato's main bodyguard.

From a distance, Oksana looked drunk, but Aiko knew better. Strong sedatives were frequently used to capture and control the young women of Masato's business.

As Oksana was placed in the taxi's back seat, a man unknown to Aiko put a silver briefcase in the trunk. Once everyone was in the cab, it left the curb, made a U-turn and then stopped at a red light a short distance from Aiko. In those moments before the light changed green, Aiko saw Oksana leaning against the taxi window. Her eyes were unfocused and vacant. Makeup on the young girl's face made her look older than her fourteen years.

Life was very different for Aiko when she was fourteen. Well educated and fluent in English by then, she was an excellent student in the disciplines of the arts. Her training included jujitsu as well as karate. During the first two years of Kenjutsu, the art of Japanese sword training, she was only allowed to use a wooden sword called a bokuto. She then advanced to one made of bamboo called a Shinai, before she trained with the katana. What she remembered most at age fourteen was her introduction and the training in an art known as Shijuhatte, better known as Kama Sutra, the art of making love.

The light changed and a horn blew as the cab sped away in the direction of Portland's waterfront. A fleeting glimpse of Aiko's image bounced off the side window of the cab.

Aiko had no money for a cab of her own, so she started running. She came upon a bicycle leaning against a light pole. As the bike owner was removing his helmet, Aiko pretended to accidentally knock it out of his hand. As he bent over to pick up it up, she jumped on his bike and sped off in the direction of the disappearing taxi.

*****

For the group of homeless people just up the street from the Japanese Tea Gardens, it would be another long night in the struggle to stay warm. The small fire at the end of their cigarettes provided more than the release of nicotine, it was heat for their cold fingers. They paid no mind to the vehicles and people passing by them, knowing those same people considered them invisible, as if this could never happen to them.

A few dimmed lights were scattered around the closed Tea Gardens, gently illuminating the rich green foliage and brilliant colored blossoms. From inside the gardens, the sound of a waterfall was light and musical, like wind chimes on a distant porch.

The taxi carrying Oksana and her predators pulled up in front of the gardens and they exited the vehicle.

From down the street, Aiko recognized the two men who walked out of the main entrance of the gardens. It was the Argentinean businessman Sergio Alvarez, and his bodyguard.

Wanting a better look at the situation, Aiko silently walked toward the gardens. She passed by three homeless men without incident. From the shadows, a fourth man grabbed her from behind and clamped his hand over her mouth. As the man pulled Aiko into the shadows with him, she raised her foot to stomp on his instep. That was when Kyle let her know it was him.

"I was about to kill you. Do not ever do that to me again," Aiko whispered ferociously.

"I didn't know how to get your attention and nobody else's."

A brief look of affection passed between Aiko and Kyle before they turned their attention back to the scene in front of the gardens. In the bodyguard's hand, was a silver briefcase, identical to the one in the taxi's trunk. One briefcase contained the winning bid and the other one, proof of purchase in the form of forged documents. As the bodyguard received the signal from Alvarez to exchange the cases, the businessman examined the still-catatonic Oksana. Satisfied with his purchase, Hitoshi handed the girl over to Alvarez.

He took her by the hand and led her through the entrance of the gardens.

"Did what I think just happened, really happen?" asked Kyle as he took Aiko's hand and pulled her away from the shadows.

"She just got sold to the highest bidder."

Aiko dropped Kyle's hand and headed across the street opposite of the gardens at a fast pace.

"Aiko, wait," Kyle said in a loud whisper.

At the sound of her name, one of the homeless men turned to look at the woman hurrying past him. Karl Bogdanoff reached into a pocket of his dirty tattered clothing and pulled out a cell phone. As he watched Kyle scurry to catch up with Aiko, he made a call to his employer. "I have eyes on her."

"Let them go, Bogdanoff, I need you here to check on some unwanted guests. Besides, they're not going anywhere."

Bogdanoff was clearly irritated with the change of plans.

Masato clarified his order. "Check on the dark sedan parked down the street."

Before he did as he was told, the killer watched Aiko and Kyle disappear down the road.

*****

188

As Kyle walked next to Aiko, he took a moment to reach out and take her by the hand.

"Where are you going, exactly?"

Aiko stopped and looked in the direction from which they just came. "What do you see?"

"The Tea Garden."

"And what is beyond that?" Aiko questioned.

Kyle paused as if it was a trick question.

Aiko continued. "The Pearl. And beyond that?"

It finally clicked with Kyle. "Red Sun Exports."

"Yes, all three of Masato's businesses align with each other and are sitting over one of the main catacombs of the Shanghai Tunnels."

"I heard they're just old basement storage areas."

"They are more than that."

Aiko headed down the road in the direction of the waterfront, a few blocks away. Kyle picked up his pace until he was side by side with her.

"Are you sure this is the way in?"

"I am sure."

"How sure? You don't even know how old these tunnels are. They could have collapsed by now."

"They have not collapsed. They have been there since the 1850's. Masato told me they were built to move the goods from the shipping docks from the Willamette River into town. They were designed to come up under the hotels, saloons, and the waterfront businesses."

"But it's my understanding they've all been shut down."

Aiko looked intensely into Kyle's eyes, "How do you think Masato has been moving his merchandise without you seeing him?"

Kyle ran his hand through his hair when he understood the implication, "Oh man, he's reopened the tunnels from the Red Sun to the waterfront."

"That is correct." Aiko smiled at his sudden realization. "Back in the days of prohibition, the drinking went underground, so did the gambling and prostitution. Masato also said people from all walks of life, from cowboys to construction workers to vagabonds, were shanghaied to work the ships. And do you know what this area used to be called in those days?"

Kyle shook his head no.

"The Unheavenly City."

Chapter 21

The night had not yet settled in, a few patrons were out strolling the streets and window shopping the local art galleries. Kyle and Aiko had just finished their 99-cent hotdogs from the local 7-11.

"Can I ask you something, Kyle? Why is it that we are only allowed mustard and relish?"

"Because anything else is just wrong," Kyle laughed.

"Are you laughing at me?"

"Never. It's hard to explain."

Kyle tossed his wrapper in the garbage. Aiko mimicked him when she made her wrapper into a ball and shot it into the trash can.

"Not bad for a girl."

"I am not a girl."

"This is true. I apologize."

He offered her a sip of his soda.

"No, thank you. It is too cold."

Kyle removed the lid, took a sip and flicked the rest of the ice out into the gutter.

Aiko looked in the cup before she took her sip. "That is all I want, thank you," she said.

Kyle finished the drink and tossed the cup in the green recycle trash barrel.

They walked close together on their way to the waterfront.

"I don't see anything," said Kyle.

"You won't."

By the expression on her face, Kyle knew Aiko was deep in thought about something. "Are you having second thoughts?"

"No, I just wanted to say, I heard you talking about your brother at the hospital. I am sorry for your loss."

"Your father killed him Aiko, and he tried to kill you to keep you from talking—"

"About the girl," Aiko said, finishing his sentence.

"Yes. Her name is Oksana. A man named Pankov made some sort of deal that somehow included my father."

"I have heard of this man, Pankov.

"The two of them are involved in human trafficking. Masato has the businessmen in his pocket and Pankov has the politicians, including our President." There was an obvious bitterness in Kyle's voice.

"What do you think he has on the President?"

"Let's sit a minute and I'll tell you what I know."

The couple sat down on a park bench. Kyle put his arm around Aiko as she rested her head on his shoulder.

"Oksana is President Dalton's daughter, not Pankov's. Back when the President was a Senator, Pankov used his wife, Karina, to set up the Senator and get him in compromising photographs. It was a way to get his hooks into him. During the blackmail session, Karina got pregnant. Years later, Pankov realized Oksana was not his, so he and Masato made a deal to sell her to the highest bidder to get her out of the country. When she was gone, so was the proof. All they needed to keep their leverage were the photos."

"So how is your father tied into this?"

"I'm not sure, but I know it has something to do with my mother."

There was worry in Aiko's voice as she asked, "How far do you think your father is willing to go to protect his career?"

"Why?"

"Do you think he would have told Masato where we were in order to send Pena to kill me?"

"At first, I thought he gave Pena our location. But, when Pena said he was there to kill both of us, I knew it couldn't have been my father."

"There could be another way they got our location."

"What did you have in mind?"

"We are being tracked. Rather, I am." Aiko showed no reaction as she spoke. "I have only suspected until now, but it could be a possibility."

"Such as?"

"I will need your help."

"Sure, what is it?"

"I need you to cut me."

"What?" Shock and bewilderment showed on Kyle's face.

"Just help me. I will do most of the work."

Aiko stood up, drew her sword and handed it to Kyle.

"Why are—?"

"Please, Kyle, take it."

He reluctantly took it by the handle as Aiko grabbed the sword near the end of the blade. She looked around. Seeing that no one was taking an interest in them, she guided the tip of the blade and laid it to rest on the inside of her forearm about halfway up.

"What are you doing?"

"Please, do not move."

Aiko placed the tip of the blade on a mark about the size of the freckle in the middle of her forearm and made a slight incision into her arm. She slowly drew the blade across her skin about half an inch before withdrawing it. A small amount of blood started to flow. Kyle put the blade back into its scabbard. He reached into his pocket and pulled out a handkerchief, trying to wipe away the blood.

Aiko pushed Kyle's hand away. "Not yet." Her fingers kept massaging her forearm below the cut until a small, thin capsule appeared, a tracking device.

As it protruded from the cut, Kyle grabbed the end of the inch-long capsule and removed it. He wiped the blood off Aiko's arm and folded the handkerchief into a bandage, pressing it against the cut. While Aiko held the handkerchief in place, Kyle studied the tiny capsule.

Aiko spoke calmly. "I have seen Masato use these before but I never knew I had one. After Masato found me at the hospital and then Pena's visit to the houseboat, we both assumed it might be your father. You don't trust him, but you still didn't think he would have given up our location to have us killed. That's when I suspected Masato must have tagged me as well."

"So, Masato knew all along where we were?"

"Maybe your father is not to blame for this."

"He's still involved somehow. He's not getting off that easy. How many girls do you think Masato has tagged?"

The conversation ceased between Kyle and Aiko when a man walking a Yorkie came within earshot.

Kyle hid the tracker in his hand as he turned his attention to the man and his dog. "Good evening."

"Good evening," replied the man.

"Cute dog. What's his name?"

"Rags."

Kyle knelt down and petted the dog. "Hey, fella." He returned his attention to the dog's owner. "How old is he?"

"Oh, he's about 16."

"Nice evening for a walk."

"It's perfect. It's been awhile since we've been to Portland."

Kyle continued to pet Rags as he casually asked, "Where you from?"

"Salem. We were here for a dog show. Now we're stretching our legs one last time before heading home."

As Kyle scratched around Rags' ears one last time, he placed the tracker in one of the holes that made up the catches for the dog's adjustable collar. "Well, it was nice to meet you, Rags." He stood up and addressed the man. "Have a safe trip back to Salem."

"Thank you. And I hope the two of you have a good evening as well."

The man and his Yorkie continued their stroll along the river. Kyle walked back to the bench.

"What did you just do?" Aiko asked.

"I talked to Rags. He is going to help us out. I put the tracker in his collar and he's going to take it to Salem for us."

"You can talk to dogs?"

"It's a gift.

Chapter 22

The magnificent horticulture of the Japanese Tea Garden went unnoticed by Oksana. If she had been alert and there for another reason, she would have commented on the large orange and white koi fish swimming in the ponds. The act of their swimming created a mesmerizing effect on anyone watching them.

Surrounding the ponds and waterfalls were expertly pruned and shaped trees and shrubs. Perfectly manicured paths to wander on led past flowers in bright colors such as Loud Pink, Snowflake White and Lemon Yellow.

Oksana was guided from Alvarez's side into a room to be prepared for his pleasure. Meanwhile, Alvarez joined Masato beneath a large arbor. They sat at a small table smoking cigars and sipping brandy. A server approached, bringing a tray of freshly prepared sushi and placed it in the center of the table facing Alvarez.

"As per your request, Mr. Alvarez," said Masato.

Also on the table were plates of cheeses, crackers, dried fruit and nuts. A silver briefcase sat open on the table.

Inside, were IDs, passports and other forged documents created for Oksana's new identity.

Alvarez scanned the paperwork. Masato assured him everything was in order. "I guarantee you, Sergio, it's all there."

"And the girl?"

"I can also promise you, she is all there as well. Her virginity is still intact. I checked on it personally," Masato said with a smug look on his face.

Alvarez glanced around as he sipped his brandy. "I see you have done very well for yourself in the export of very rare acquisitions."

"I have many sources and new ones are available to us every day. I am sure you will be very happy with this latest addition. In fact, she is one of a kind. As you know, it is not every day you come across an example with such a family pedigree as this one. Should you, in the future, request something with the same quality of standards, I am sure we will do our best to fulfill your request. Do you have a preference on which century?"

"The earlier the better. Can you find something maybe from the 12th century?"

Masato was pleased with Alvarez's interest to do business with him again. "I am sure we can arrange that for you."

"Then I look forward to seeing you again and doing some more business with you very soon, Ichiro-san."

"As long as you keep to the arrangements we agreed upon. Today's purchase will stay in South America in your collection, permanently."

Alvarez closed his briefcase then raised his brandy glass as a salute to Masato. "Here's to young love."

Masato raised his glass in the same fashion to Alvarez. "Salute."

After the toast, Masato took the flag pin from his pocket that Oksana had worn and wedged it into a nutcracker, crushing it beyond recognition.

"Whoops." Masato laughed at his action.

Alvarez arrogantly smiled in agreement.

*****

On the way to the dock, Kyle said, "Aiko, wait. Tell me where we're going."

An old floating dock, weathered by the tough demands of the busy waterway, extended roughly twenty-five yards out into the Willamette River. On the shore, near the base of the dock, was a spillway coming out of a large metal tube.

"This is actually an offshoot of one of the original tunnels," Aiko explained. "We don't have much time and this is the only way we can get in." Aiko glanced fervently around as she continued the last hundred feet toward the dock. Pointing to the tunnel entrance as she explained to Kyle, "This end of the tunnel leads back to the tea gardens, the nightclub and Masato's offices."

Kyle's gaze shifted from Aiko to the large rusty grate guarding the tunnel. "It looks pretty old. Are you sure this is the best way in?"

"It is our only way in." Aiko reached behind the grate and pulled the hidden lever. The grate opened with such a shriek it rattled Kyle's teeth, as well as his nerves.

"Why are you doing this?" asked Kyle.

Aiko turned and gave him a penetrating stare. "No one deserves what is about to happen to Oksana." She touched his arm. "Do you know why you are doing this? If you don't, you will not make it out."

Kyle returned Aiko's touch then checked the clip in his gun. Aiko checked her sword, making sure it was strapped securely to her side. The detective leaned in and gave her a kiss. "That's for luck."

"Luck will have nothing to do with it."

Aiko countered Kyle's token of affection with another kiss. "That is for you."

As they entered the tunnel, the sun was setting on the horizon. The neon lights of the Pearl District began coming on, and they painted one of Portland's eclectic cityscapes.

Chapter 23

Oksana was not able to stand by herself. A short, but well-built guard supported her from behind with his hands beneath her arms. The dose of Rohypnol that the guard had given her earlier kept Oksana submissive and blurred her vision. There was no shortage of Ruffies to be found behind the scenes of The Pearl. Masato used them as a way to help control the girls and begin the brain-washing techniques that changed them into their new personas. Oksana tried to focus on her surroundings, but could see only distorted shapes.

Tamika, a handsome Japanese woman, had been given a choice, be sold or to go into indentured servitude for Masato. As part of the brainwashing technique, he always gave them a choice. A psychological maneuver, giving the girls the illusion they had a say in the matter.

Tamika moved around in the room lighting candles that were nestled in tall, ornate candle-holders. Handmade drapes with brilliantly colored designs of cherry blossoms in full bloom hung on the walls. The room itself contained a minimal amount of furniture: a four-poster king size bed, a chair, a round table, and a bookshelf. Hidden in the bookshelf was something special, a camera.

Masato had installed a high-definition camera so that he could keep an eye on his guests. He used the recorded sessions as blackmail to keep their silence.

"Hallo?" Oksana's words were slurred and thick. No amount of swallowing helped to relieve her dry mouth. She wanted to rub the fuzziness from her eyes but found she couldn't move her arms.

Tamika quickly finished lighting the three remaining candles then scurried over to Oksana.

"We must get you ready for your new master," the servant said. "We don't want to disappoint him." She picked up a black silk robe, embroidered with white long-stemmed roses, that was lying on the bed and walked over to Oksana.

"Please, I must dress you in this," Tamika said as she held the silk robe for the young captive to see.

"Where am I?" the confused girl mumbled.

"Must hurry," Tamika said as she laid the robe on the bed and started removing Oksana's t-shirt.

Trying to push away Tamika's hands proved to be futile for Oksana.

Rohypnol, also known as "the date rape drug," seemed to have tentacles that kept pulling her back into the depths of a black void.

Once Oksana was wearing the robe, the guard guided her to the king size bed and laid her down. Tamika tied silk scarves to each of Oksana's wrists and then tied the scarves to the bedposts. On the nightstand, the guard had set up a small black case. From the case, he took out an injection gun and slipped the large gauge needle into Oksana's forearm. It only took a second to shoot the small tracker capsule under her skin. The capsule, known as an RFID, is a sub-dermal radio-frequency identification chip. A small antenna in a tiny glass tube is less than a half an inch long and no wider than a strand of boiled spaghetti. The chip is a satellite-enabled tracking device that relays a signal to any GPS device that has the program to track the designated frequency.

After removing the needle, the guard placed a small circular Band-Aid over the puncture mark. His task was finished, and Tamika was close to completing hers. She reached up under the silk robe and removed Oksana's underwear, placing them on the nightstand.

Tamika stepped back from the bed and surveyed the display before her.

Small tears collected in the corners of her eyes as she remembered being in the same position and having to make a choice. Her heart ached for the frightening pain this innocent girl would soon experience.

Before leaving, Tamika checked to make sure everything was in place. On the nightstand sat bottled water and a fresh towel. A men's terry cloth bathrobe hung from the hook on the back of the door. The small table in the corner had a washbasin with a pitcher of fresh water next to it. Tamika and the guard left the room and locked the door behind them, leaving the key in the lock.

*****

Kyle stood in the tunnel, his eyes trying to adjust to the dim light. Behind him were the faint sounds of Aiko descending a rusty metal ladder. When she was by his side he asked her, "How does it look?"

"Clear for now, we must hurry."

Kyle followed Aiko as she went back up the ladder. At the top, Aiko quietly lifted and put to the side, a hatch cover that blended in with its surroundings. The couple found themselves behind several rock pillars of various sizes and shapes. In front of the pillars was a small pond, its surface calm and smooth.

The rock sculpture reflected in the unusually blue water of the pond a 3-D illusion. It was designed to be viewed in such a manner for its full effect.

From behind the sculpture, Aiko and Kyle emerged, their senses on high alert as they made their way to the path leading to the room where Oksana was held captive.

*****

With her head slightly bowed, Aiko approached Oksana's room. The guard in front of the door momentarily forgot about the cigarette in his hand as he admired the beautiful woman walking toward him. He dropped the cigarette at his feet and glanced down to crush it under the tip of his shoe. Just as he looked up, and before he could react, Aiko silently ran her katana through him. As she withdrew the blade, the guard fell to his knees. Her hand immediately covered his mouth to prevent him from making any noise. The guard's last gasp of air was warm as it slipped through her fingers.

Kyle appeared from the opposite direction and quickly unlocked Oksana's door. He and Aiko pulled the dead guard into the room. Seeing Oksana tied to the bed and barely conscious, Kyle let the guard drop to the floor with a thud.

As they untied the young girl from the bed, Kyle noticed the small Band-Aid on the inside of her forearm. He peeled it off and helped Aiko use the same technique to extract the tracking device from Oksana that she had used earlier to remove one from herself earlier. Taking the towel from the nightstand, she tore off a few strips, folding one into a bandage and using the other to tie makeshift gauze in place to help stop the bleeding.

Pressed for time, Aiko picked up Oksana's underwear and shoved them in the front pocket of her jeans. She and Kyle then put one of the girl's arms over each of their shoulders as they made their way back to the tunnel entrance by the rock sculpture. Before entering the tunnel, Aiko dipped her hand into the pool of cold water and rubbed it over Oksana's face, hoping it would help revive the catatonic girl. The second time Aiko reached into the pond for water, the ripples distorted the reflection of Oksana's face, mirroring the girl's confusion.

*****

A block from the Japanese Tea Garden, two FBI agents, Cabral and Caceres, sat in an unmarked car, watching the entrance to the gardens.

They scarcely noticed the homeless man with the small scar under his right eye pushing a shopping cart past their car. Their attention was focused on the activity displayed on the laptop in front of them. On the screen was a map showing one red blinking dot. The dot was located within the confines of the tea garden and was not moving.

Just as Cabral's cell phone rang, the stationary red dot on the laptop monitor disappeared.

"This is Cabral. . . Yeah, Caceres spotted Morrell's kid, Kyle, up the block, so we're waiting to see what happens next. We just lost the signal for Red Butterfly. Its last transmission came from inside the gardens. Yes, sir. We've been monitoring Morrell's cell phone and it's been fading in and out, but we know he's close. Yes, sir." Cabral disconnected the call.

Caceres glanced over at Cabral. "How old is Red Butterfly?"

"Fourteen, I think. Really doesn't matter. We were told only to observe and not engage."

"Guess you're right. If you don't officially exist, who's going to miss you when you're gone?"

Caceres, who was sitting in the passenger seat, put a U-shaped travel pillow around his stiff neck. "That last flight out of SFO was a killer. You keep watch for a while." Caceres settled in and closed his eyes. In a voice, well on its way to being thick with sleep, he asked, "By the way, who came up with Red Butterfly?"

"The word came down that she could be the daughter of the President and her mother is Russian," Cabral replied.

"What? That would go all the way back when he was a Senator."

"Then that makes sense."

"If this turns out to be true, the talks they are having right now in Russia will be compromised," Caceres yawned and within seconds was lightly snoring.

Cabral shook his head and grinned, then turned his attention towards the bum with a shopping cart headed in his direction. "Wonder what this yahoo wants," he muttered under his breath as the homeless man stopped his cart directly across from their car.

Bogdanoff, expertly dressed as a bum, put his foot up onto a short wall that paralleled the sidewalk.

He pretended to tie his old bootstraps as he let go of the cart, letting it roll toward the driver's side door of the agents' car. Cabral saw the cart headed toward him and rolled down his window. "Hey buddy, you're losing your cart."

Bogdanoff turned and reached for the handle of the cart with one hand and with his other, reached under the edge of the large piece of cardboard covering the top of his cart. The cart, filled with empty plastic bottles, was the perfect cover to hide the 12-gauge shotgun he had pointed at the agent's head. To help mute the sound of a shotgun blast, Bogdanoff had placed one of the plastic two-liter bottles on the end of a single barreled shotgun to use as a silencer.

Cabral was about to speak to the bum again when the shotgun went off, killing him and Caceres with one shot.

The window on the passenger side of the car blew out, followed by a mass exit of little white beads of Styrofoam. A blotch of red Styrofoam landed near the opposite curb with a light splat, followed by a soft snowfall of white beads coming down over the top of it.

To make sure the job was complete, Bogdanoff took out his .22 pistol with a silencer and double tapped the two agents in their chests.

He took a quick look around to make sure there were no witnesses. He reached in the car window and grabbed the FBI-issued laptop, and stashed it in his cart before pushing the cart back in the direction from which he came.

Next to the blotch of red stained Styrofoam was a gutter drain opening. A large rat appeared from just inside the edge of the drain and eyed the red mass. A light gust of wind sent some of the white beads of Styrofoam toward the hungry rodent. The white pellets bounced off its mangled fur, startled it and sent it running. More white foam beads tossed around by the night air made the rat scurry back down the drain from where it came.

Chapter 24

The trip back down the tunnel ladder was arduous for Oksana. Although she was finally emerging from her drug-induced state, her limbs still felt uncoordinated and heavy. The thick fog in her brain was taking its time to evaporate. Oksana had not yet fully realized what a serious situation from which she had just been rescued. Nor had she been able to process exactly who the two people were that were helping her down a ladder.

Once Kyle, Aiko and Oksana cleared the ladder, Kyle wrapped his arm around Oksana to hold her steady as Aiko knelt down to help her put her underwear back on.

The girls stood close to the wall while Kyle checked up and down the tunnel for possible danger. Satisfied no one was nearby, the detective started walking in the direction he and Aiko had originally come from.

"C'mon, it's going to be daylight soon," Kyle urged.

Aiko didn't move. She pointed in the opposite direction and said to Kyle, "We need to go this way."

"But the water is this way."

"Yes, but the tanto is the other way. It is the only thing that is keeping us alive. I know where it is and it is our only way out." Aiko's voice was firm and determined.

"You've known all this time and never said anything?"

Aiko sighed, "I just learned of its whereabouts recently. It is the only leverage we have if we want to get out of this situation alive. Masato does not tolerate defeat. And in his eyes, losing me and Oksana is considered defeat."

"What is it about this sword?"

"This sword may not have any meaning to you but it is one of three swords that represent our family's legacy. To have the set restored as one would be a priceless treasure." Aiko gave Kyle a heartfelt look. "Until you find what gives your life meaning, you too will be lost."

Kyle could see Aiko was on a mission and not just for the sword, but for Oksana as well.

Not waiting for a response from Kyle, Aiko grabbed Oksana by the hand and pulled her in the opposite direction of the way out and to safety, but instead, toward her former home.

As the tunnel started to narrow, so did Kyle's thoughts. Aiko had touched on something, something that he had not realized.

Oksana was a part of him long before he met her. She was a way to accept and forgive a part of his past that had been haunting him for a long time.

*****

There wasn't much conversation as the three of them continued through the dim narrow tunnel. With each step, Oksana seemed to be regaining more strength. As they continued through the tunnel, the musty air surrounded them like a thick blanket, making it harder to breathe. The further they walked, the stronger the vibrations around them became. With each step, a rhythm developed, like a precursor to a dance.

Oksana stopped in her tracks. "I hear music."

"We are coming to the part of the tunnel that passes directly under Masato's nightclub," Aiko replied.

"What else does he own along this tunnel besides the nightclub, the tea garden and the Red Sun Exports?" Kyle asked.

"He owns a couple of restaurants and a few retail shops. But none of those businesses are along this leg of the tunnel. These are the only three that he needs to have isolated so that he and his men are able to move the girls undetected."

215

Kyle hated to ask Aiko, but he needed confirmation of his suspicions. "You were a part of this, Masato's human trafficking ring?"

Shame was evident in both Aiko's eyes and voice as she softly answered. "Yes, but only because I was in a position where there was nothing I could do to stop it. My allegiance was to my master and I obeyed."

Immediately Kyle regretted asking her the question, especially in front of Oksana. His feelings had gotten the best of him, and he was having a hard time understanding the culture that she was brought up in, even in these modern times. He reached out to her, put his hand around the back of her neck, leaned in and gave her a light kiss on her forehead.

"Well, now you don't have to obey anyone. You are now the master of your own life."

Aiko smiled. They looked into each other's eyes, each sensing a shared healing between them.

The small group continued down the tunnel when suddenly, Aiko reached out and stopped Oksana from going any further. They were coming upon an alcove that had barely enough light to reflect the shards of glass that had been planted in the ground.

They looked like rows and rows of shark's teeth with varying sizes and angles, designed to discourage anyone from trying to escape.

"What is this all about?" Kyle asked.

"See the box over there?" Aiko replied.

"The one with all the old shoes?" queried Oksana.

"Yes. All of this has been here for a very long time. They used to remove the shoes of the people they were holding down here. They kept them in the dark and used the glass as a deterrent to keep them from leaving."

"Oksana, stay along the wall and you'll be fine," Kyle instructed.

After the trio maneuvered around the glass in the floor, they reached an area where two stacked mattresses laid on the floor just below a trap door. Two light fixtures hung about five feet apart, each with a single bulb. Each fixture was bolted to a long two-by-four and attached to the ceiling of the tunnel. This set-up provided the only ambiance besides the loud music leaking down through the trap door.

Unfortunately, the loud music did more than cover up any noise Kyle, Aiko and Oksana made in the tunnel, it also camouflaged the movements of two of Masato's men.

Caught off guard, Aiko and Kyle found themselves in a fight that nearly ended before it began.

One of the men grabbed Aiko from behind and threw her hard into the brick-lined wall. He took a swing at her with the intention of knocking her out with one swift blow to the jaw. She managed to move enough to avoid the full contact of the man's fist as it glanced off her chin, but she was momentarily left breathless as he delivered a second blow to her midsection. His punch slammed her back up against the wall for the second time.

Kyle drew his weapon on the second man. As he brought up the gun, his assailant stepped to the side. Before Kyle had time to react, the man grabbed his wrist and twisted inward and up. The pain was too much for him to hang onto the gun. As Kyle's arm was torqued upward, his hand flew open, the momentum causing him to release his firearm from his grasp. The gun flew through the air, taking out one of the tunnel lights and left just one bulb to cast their silhouettes on the walls. The assailant pivoted on his heel and rotated his hips, connecting his knee to Kyle's chest and knocked him to the ground, causing a few moments of disorientation for the detective.

Kyle's attacker then turned his attention to Oksana. Confused and paralyzed with fear, all the young girl could do was clinch the lapels of her robe and pull her fists tightly together over her heart. The menacing figure gripped her arm. It was then that Oksana found her voice and screamed.

Just a few yards away, Aiko's fury and martial arts training were on full autopilot as she held her own with her assailant. She managed to kick the man just above his knee, buckling his leg, which gave her enough time to pull out her sword. As she did, Aiko misjudged the small tunnel space, so when she thrust her sword at her opponent's midsection, all she accomplished was a glancing blow off the side of his ribs. Her thrust of the sword only pierced the man's loose shirt. The tip of her sword tore away a piece of it, lodging it and the tip of her sword into a large railroad tie used as a vertical support beam. This action was done with such force that the katana was jammed in the wooden beam and she was unable to retrieve it. The katana's blade was left parallel to the ground with the blade's razor-sharp edge facing the action.

Kyle, back on his feet, gave his opponent a shot to the kidneys from behind. At the same time, Oksana bit the man on his forearm.

He released her and delivered a backhand across Oksana's face, knocking her to the ground.

With both hands free, Masato's man hit Kyle in the ribs, dropping him to his knees. While doubled over, Kyle grabbed a handful of dirt off the tunnel floor and threw it in his attacker's face. In the few seconds his opponent was blinded. Kyle kicked him between the legs, the man lost his breath and fell to his knees. Kyle front-kicked his opponent in the chest. The man flew backward and landed flat his back, directly on top of the rows of glass shards. His screams seemed to go on forever down the tunnel. He managed to pull himself off the ground, unaware glass was still sticking out of his back. The severe pain produced a trance-like state in the man, yet he had enough awareness to go after the person who caused his agony. With his remaining strength, he charged at Kyle. The detective grabbed his attacker and threw him back onto the top mattress.

The fight between Aiko and Masato's man had reached an impasse until her attacker used a maneuver that caught Aiko off balance. The man grabbed her from behind and pushed her toward the sword that was jammed in the railroad tie. He bull rushed her toward the katana's cutting edge.

Aiko used every martial arts technique taught to her, and then some, but her opponent was bigger and stronger.

Seeing Aiko being pushed toward the sword, Kyle searched frantically in the dim light for his gun. It wasn't where he thought it was.

Kyle turned and saw Oksana pointing his gun at the man lying on top of the mattresses. The man wasn't moving, but it didn't matter. Aiko was running out of time.

Reaching his hand out towards the young girl, Kyle said, "The gun please, Oksana."

Nervous and a bit shaky, Oksana drifted over next to Kyle and handed him the gun. The attacker tried to take advantage of the situation by stealthily standing up. His action was a mistake because he put himself in the line of fire between Kyle and Aiko's assailant.

Shrugging his shoulders, Kyle said, "If you insist," and fired. The man fell back onto the mattress, dead.

The echo of the shot was so loud it startled Aiko's attacker. This was enough for her to break free and move to the side before being pushed into the blade. Just as Kyle aimed his gun at Aiko's opponent, the fight's momentum changed, as did their positions.

Aiko had her back to Kyle, blocking the larger man. With his strength, the attacker was able to grip the katana by the handle with both hands, and pull it free from the railroad tie. Aiko knew the last remaining light was at her back and that gave her an advantage. The man could not see her eyes. She slowly stepped back, drawing him in closer to the brightness of the light's luminescence. When she was right below the light bulb, she stopped.

"Say goodnight, sweetheart," the man snarled.

Aiko reached up, and with a little three-quarter turn, unscrewed the remaining light bulb from its white porcelain insulated socket. With that slight turn of her wrist, and the *eeek* that filled the tunnel, it sent the area around them into total darkness. Kyle and Oksana held their breath as they heard the man charge at Aiko with a growling battle cry from deep within. "Ahhhh . . ."

What followed was one of those moments of silence that felt like an eternity before Kyle heard any noise. It was the assailant, quietly moving about, searching the darkness for his prey. Kyle knew his advances were not missed by Aiko's senses. Then came the sounds of crushing blows to the man's ribs and his harsh moans reverberated in the small space.

Oksana let out a small gasp before Kyle, close enough to find her in the dark, put his hand over her mouth and whispered, "Shhh," in her ear. There were a series of "swooshes" as the blade of the katana cut through the air searching for its target. Silence once again, as everyone waited for someone else to make a mistake.

All of the action had amped up the enemy's breathing. Just as Kyle homed in on him, Aiko's fist located the man's windpipe, crushing it. The katana hit the ground, spinning out of control like a quarter about to land flat on a table. The ringing noise from the blade of the katana suddenly stopped.

Kyle knew Aiko had the sword within her grasp. The man could not hide his labored breathing from Aiko. There was the sound of a *swoosh,* followed by a thump, then the thud of the man's headless body falling to the ground.

Kyle called out into the darkness for Aiko. All he could hear was his own heart pounding out of his chest. That's when he heard the light bulb being screwed back into its socket, *"eeek."* Relief washed over him and Oksana as they saw Aiko. Except for her tattered clothes and messy hair, she appeared to be relatively unharmed.

The worst appeared to be a small amount of blood dripping from minor cuts around her face. Most evident of Aiko's condition though, was the victorious smile on her face and the blood-stained sword in her hand.

Chapter 25

The ambiance of a full moon created a picturesque scene as its light filled the central courtyard of the tea garden. In the distance, a small waterfall fed a brook that made its way under the arch of a wooden footbridge. At the edge of the brook, two turtles rested on a flat rock, still faintly warm from the sun's rays earlier that afternoon. Blossoms from the Japanese maple trees cast night shadows over the manicured lawns. The colors and shapes of the tea garden were perfect exhibits of serenity. Tall bamboo stalks swayed in the wind, and scents from the garden flowers were reminiscent of a long rich Japanese history. A woman played soothing sounds originating from a Japanese stringed musical instrument called a koto. Its mollifying music blended with the cordial conversation between Sergio and Masato.

In between smoking cigars and drinking brandy, the men shared their personal sexual conquest stories.

After a bit, Sergio said, "I paid nearly double for this girl, how can I be sure she is who you say she is?"

Masato's icy stare gave Sergio a chill up the hardened businessman's spine. "Are you questioning my word?"

"Ichiro-san, it's just—" Sergio stopped mid-sentence as Masato slid a closed file into the center of the table that was given to him by Pankov.

"This contains a sample of the President's DNA from when he was a Senator. It also contains the results of a sample from the girl's DNA from last year. It proves they are a familial match.

"I was not trying to insult you, Ichiro-san, I was just asking for your word."

The tension was briefly broken. Then Masato saw Tamika approach from a distance with a look of concern on her face. She walked quickly along the precision stone path and passed by a shrine of Buddha made from stone. The Buddha sat in the middle of a Zen garden. Rows of sand were perfectly raked in a circular pattern around a series of granite rocks that decorated the open space of the garden.

Tamika stopped at Masato's side and whispered in his ear. "Ichiro-san, the girl is gone." Masato's anger was immediate and intense. He displayed his frustration with a swift backhand to his drink, sending it flying off the table and it splashed all over Tamika's beautiful kimono.

"Find her!" he roared.

"What is going on, Masato?" A concerned Sergio asked.

By now, Masato was on his feet. First, he looked at his client then he focused on his bodyguard Hitoshi's eyes.

"Mr. Alvarez, I'm afraid I'm going to have to void our contract."

Just as Sergio was about to comment, Hitoshi drew his gun and shot Alvarez's bodyguard point-blank. The silencer on the gun was still smoking when Hitoshi cracked off two more rounds into the heart of Alvarez.

*****

The recent battle with Masato's men had left Aiko, Kyle and Oksana, physically and emotionally on edge. They continued through the tunnel with Aiko in the lead. They stopped to rest by a small alcove after twenty minutes of hazardous walking through the dimly lit tunnel. The alcove was opposite an old wooden staircase that ascended to a hatch leading to Red Sun Exports. Along the edge of the alcove's low ceiling was a strand of small clear lights. They created just enough shadows to play tricks with your eyes and give you an eerie feeling of being watched.

The alcove was only large enough for a standard size bed, an antique dresser with a large mirror attached to the back of it, and a nightstand next to the bed.

"Why is there a bed in the tunnel, Aiko?" Kyle asked as he opened the dresser and checked the contents of the cabinet drawers.

"Why do you think?" Aiko replied.

Oksana's small voice was getting stronger, "Where are we?"

"We are right below Red Sun Exports."

They sat on the edge of the bed with Oksana between them. After a quick examination of her arm, Oksana said, "What happened to my arm?"

"It was nothing," Kyle answered, his voice casual and distracted.

Aiko gave Kyle a disapproving look before giving the girl an explanation. "It was a way for Masato to track you, Oksana."

"He was going to sell me, wasn't he?"

"Yes," Aiko said softly.

Kyle's voice sounded optimistic as he said, "But now you don't have to worry about anything like that ever again."

"Is it true, my father is the President?"

"From what your mother told me, I'm pretty sure that's true," Kyle answered.

"Does he even know about me?"

"I don't think he did until recently."

"Why doesn't he want me?"

"That is what your mom was trying to do, get you to him."

Oksana slumped and started to cry. Kyle awkwardly put his arm around her.

"Why did they have to kill her?"

"There's a lot to tell you about your mother and father, but first we have to get you out of here."

Oksana pointed at Aiko. "Who is she?"

"This is my friend, Aiko. She knows this place very well and as you can see, she is willing to fight to protect you, so you can trust her too."

"Aiko?"

"Yes."

Oksana pointed to Kyle and asked, "Who is he?"

"This is Kyle. He is a very brave man and you can trust him too."

"Oksana," Kyle said, "you remember the man who was helping you and your mother get away from Victor?"

"Yes."

"That was my brother, Steven."

"He tried to save my mother. I shouldn't have run away."

Aiko responded with words of encouragement. "We're not running anymore."

"Why do you fight with a sword?"

"This is a katana, and I have been training for a day just like today since I was your age."

"Can you teach me?"

Aiko was hesitant as she replied, "I don't think..."

Kyle arched his eyebrows at Aiko as Oksana gave her a pleading look.

"I don't think I am the one to be teaching you, but when we get out of here, we can talk about it."

Kyle gestured toward the ladder. "I'm going to take a little look around and see if it will be dark enough for us to go soon. I'll be right back."

Kyle checked his gun and saw that there was a round in the chamber. He handed it to Aiko. "Just in case it's not me coming back down that ladder."

Aiko reluctantly took the gun and watched Kyle ascend the ladder.

Oksana tugged on Aiko's sleeve. "Aiko?"

"Yes?"

"Is he coming back?"

"Yes. He is an honorable man. He will come back for us."

Oksana looked around and didn't like what she saw. She grabbed one of the pillows and a blanket, then dropped to the floor and slipped herself under the bed.

Aiko had a moment to reflect and put herself into a Zen-like state. The moment didn't last very long as she heard the hatch above the ladder open. She looked at the gun on the bed. She felt at peace and had a sense she was not frightened. Then she saw Kyle come down the ladder.

"Where's Oksana?"

Aiko pointed under the bed. "She's tired. She needs some rest."

"She's been through a lot. We can let her rest until it's clear enough we can go up, get into Masato's office, and recover the katana."

Aiko laid back and offered Kyle the space on the bed next to her, "You could use some rest too."

"I'll be fine."

"No, you won't."

Kyle looked deep into Aiko's eyes and felt a connection he thought he would never find again.

Aiko saw something was holding him back. "You know more about my journey than I about yours. Tell me what it was that clouded your life."

"Clouded my life?"

"Yes. I can see you have a deep, dark cloud that is causing you so much pain. It is controlling your life instead of you being at peace."

Aiko put her hand over Kyle's heart. Kyle could feel the love they had shared as one from the night before. He could see the vulnerability Aiko allowed Kyle to see in her eyes. She was one who knew about the darkness one man could do to another.

They both could feel Kyle exhale a deep breath. "Are you sure you want to know?"

"Yes."

"Even if what I did caused the death of an innocent girl?"

Chapter 26

Under the bed, Oksana was awake. She had been listening to the only two people she had come to trust.

"Kyle, you did not judge me for who I am or my past. I will honor that with you."

Kyle put his head down into his hands as if to see something awful from his past. Instead, what he saw was Oksana looking back at him from under the bed. Oksana could see the anguish on his face. She crawled out from under the bed and sat next to Kyle.

When he let his mind go back to that time, he started to sense the warmth of the blood that was on his hands from the day that changed his life forever.

"I had a partner. Her name was Rachel. We had been assigned together for a couple of years and had grown pretty close. That kind of friendship where you could start to read each other's minds and finish each other's sentences. What wasn't talked about were the feelings that we were starting to feel for each other."

"She was beautiful?"

"Yes, smart too. She was getting to know me better than I knew myself. We had been working with a confidential informant on a new lead that had a lot of potential. It was tied to an illegal export business downtown."

"Does this have to do with where we are now?"

"At the time, we didn't know the connection. Over time I think it did, but I was never able to prove it."

"And you have been trying to prove it ever since?"

"Yes."

"What happened to her?"

"My partner and I were running late for, what on the surface, was a pretty straightforward undercover sting. We had a kilo of coke on loan from the police evidence locker that we were going to exchange for some small arms. We had gotten stuck behind a school bus at a railroad crossing. Just as the tracks cleared, I got a call from my dad, but I couldn't take it because we were already late and about to make the bust. I could see our guy off in the distance, waiting for us in a dirt lot, pacing by his car. As we drove up, we knew something was wrong. He was sweating and talking in a panic."

*****

Scott Olsen, a felon with a rap sheet as long as his Bermuda shorts, had worked himself into a frenzy as he paced, checking his watch every thirty seconds. After ten minutes, it must have seemed like a lifetime for the poor guy. As it turned out, a life was on the line.

As Kyle and Rachel pulled up in their unmarked car they noticed there was a man in the back seat of Scott's car. He had been shot and was bleeding out. They had noticed the gun dangling in Scott's hand but didn't overreact.

Kyle's instincts had told him to go for his gun, but he held back. Rachel had already drawn hers and slipped it down behind her hip in case things started to go sideways.

Kyle tried to assess the situation as fast as he could. "What's going on, Scotty?"

"I got a call. It's not good, man." Scotty's voice was breaking up. "Cops."

Kyle and Rachel looked at each other and slowly shook their heads.

Rachel kept her voice low and tried to get Scotty to calm down. "What do you mean, cops? Who called you?"

"I don't know who it was but he said I was being set up and he would let me know who it was by calling the guy." Scotty shook the gun in his hand in the direction of the man in the backseat of his car. "So I shot him."

"Why?"

"His phone rang, man."

"You shot a guy just because his phone rang? I thought he was your partner?"

"I really didn't know the guy at all. We were told to bring the goods here and make the deal. I had heard he was the nephew of some guy. Turns out he was a cop!"

Scotty went over to the front passenger seat, reached in the open window, pulled a MAC-10 from off a pile of weapons on the seat, racked the bolt back and then pointed it in the back seat at the young Asian man who was unaware his life was about to end without notice.

Kyle and Rachel started to move in but in an instant, Scotty whirled and pointed the MAC in their direction, stopping them in their tracks.

Kyle stepped in front of Rachel. "Hey, Scotty. Take it easy. Nobody is moving. Relax."

"Relax! I just killed a guy and you're telling me to relax!"

Rachel looked over at the man in the back seat of Scotty's car and saw he wasn't dead. "Hey Scotty, no one's dead yet. Look, he's still alive. Let us call it in and get this guy some help."

"What did you say?" Scotty's tone was all of a sudden very cool.

Kyle had heard it too. Rachel had made a second mistake. She drew her gun earlier and moved into a backup position like she had been taught in the academy. Kyle didn't think Scotty had noticed. What Scotty did notice was the way she used the phrase, "*Let us call it in.*" That's cop-talk all the way.

What seemed like slow motion happened in an instant. Kyle lunged at Scotty just as he pulled the trigger on the fully-automatic MAC-10.

Bullets ripped from the weapon, sending a small burst of lead terror at over a thousand rounds a minute, from the modified hand-held killing machine.

All Kyle could feel was his head spinning as he found himself face down in the dirt. His head was pounding and bleeding from where Scotty had cracked him over the back of the head with his MAC. Kyle looked over and saw Rachel leaning against their unit clutching her right thigh. One round had grazed her but a second had ripped into her mid-thigh. While Kyle was gathering his senses, he could make out Scotty forcing Rachel to the back end of his car. He heard some commotion, then the trunk closed.

Kyle caught something out of the corner of his eye. Rachel's gun was on the ground just a few feet away by the back tire of their unit. All he could think was that she must have dropped it when she was shot, and Scotty never saw it. Kyle's reflexes kicked in and without any hesitation, he rolled over and grabbed the gun. He had it trained on Scotty just as he poked his head out from the back end of his car.

"Drop it." Kyle's disarming request was acknowledged.

Scotty dropped the assault rifle. Kyle motioned with the Beretta to have him step away from the end of the car.

As he moved back toward the driver's side window, Kyle had one more request. "The keys. Toss them to me."

Scotty tossed the keys up in a high arch hoping Kyle's eyes would follow. When the keys hit their highest point, Scotty whirled and reached into the front seat for another gun. Kyle hadn't fallen for the trick and fired one round into the back of Scotty's thigh that dropped him to his knees. "How does it feel?"

Kyle grabbed the keys and was able to stand, but hadn't fully gotten his feet under him. He did have enough feeling in his legs to make his way to the back of the car. He used the fob to open the trunk and saw Rachel was okay.

They shared a look that didn't need any words. They knew right then they didn't want to waste any more time worrying about what others in the department might think about the feelings for one another that they had been holding back. Then they both heard the Asian man in the back seat yell out. "No!"

Kyle only got a glance as he quickly peeked around the open trunk lid and saw that Scotty had made it to his feet and had a gun pointed at the Asian man. Scotty changed his aim toward Kyle and fired. His shot went astray. Scotty then fired two rounds into the open trunk lid. He wasn't sure if he hit his mark but what he was sure of, was that Rachel was still in the trunk.

He used another round to shoot the Asian man, whose body ended up lurching over, exposing the back of the seat.

Scotty went mad and began firing into the back of the seat, sending one round after another into and through the trunk area. As the echo of the last round dissipated, Scotty saw the slide on his gun was locked back, indicating he was empty.

Kyle was crouched down on his knees below the bumper. As he took a look into the trunk he saw Rachel's body twitching. He couldn't tell how many times she had been hit but she was still alive. The life was not yet drained from her body but it wasn't good. He saw the fire and pain in her eyes from what she was feeling throughout her body, because of the few rounds that had assaulted her.

"Hold on, Rachel. I need to call this in. I'll be right back."

Kyle knew she didn't have much time and he had to risk it. He took a peek from under the car and saw Scotty hobbling away from the car. Kyle stood with a single mission on is mind, kill this bastard and save the woman he loved.

As Kyle stood up, he had to take a moment to get his bearings because, from the blow to the head he found himself experiencing vertigo. He began to follow in Scotty's direction. When he felt he had him in range, he raised his gun, locked onto his target and fired. Scotty flinched but didn't go down.

Kyle refocused, zeroed in once again, and squeezed off another round. Again, Scotty was still walking away.

The one thing that was happening was, Kyle was getting closer. Then something odd happened, Scotty stopped in his tracks and turned to face Kyle, like he was giving up. That was when Kyle threw protocol out the window and squeezed off another two rounds, dropping Scotty right where he stood.

The next thing Kyle saw was the one of the things that changed his life forever. Twenty yards ahead of where Scotty's body laid, he saw a young girl lying on the ground, dead.

*****

Kyle felt the sadness he experienced that day all over again. That feeling of being broken all the way down to his soul as he sat next to Aiko on the bed. Aiko had tears in her eyes, sympathizing with his pain.

Kyle continued, "By the time the ambulance arrived, it was all over. Because of my actions, I lost my partner and killed an eleven-year-old girl."

Aiko forced out a few words. "Rachel was more than just your partner…"

"I lost everything that day."

"Some things that are lost are usually not that far away. All it takes is a reason to find them and to bring them back into your life."

After a long pause, Aiko could tell Kyle had come to an understanding of what had been haunting him for so long, it was himself.

Kyle took a deep breath, as if God had touched his shoulder and he felt His mercy. It didn't take away the pain but he was no longer a prisoner of his own madness. "Oksana?" The mere mention of her name was like finding a missing piece of the puzzle.

Aiko saw relief with each breath Kyle took. "Yes, Kyle. You are forgiven."

It all came to him with such clarity. "If that girl had lived, she would be the same age as Oksana is now."

"Now you find yourself in a place in your life that once tore you apart, giving you a chance to make yourself whole again. That is forgiveness."

Suddenly, there was the noise of a hatch being unlocked. Aiko raised her finger to her lips with a silent "Shhh," and then touched her fingertip to Oksana's lips.

On the other side of the tunnel and above the trio, a hatch opened and a bright light shot into the tunnel. Aiko quickly pulled up the blanket and checked under the bed. She indicated to Oksana to crawl under it, which she did without any further encouragement. Once she was under, Aiko hastily slipped the sword underneath the bed to Oksana.

Grabbing a pillow off the bed, she instructed Kyle to follow her lead. From under the bed, Oksana could hear Kyle and Aiko getting undressed. She saw Kyle's pants fall to the ground, bunching around his ankles. Aiko's white shirt and red t-shirt were next. She then quickly dropped to her knees in front of Kyle.

The couple was scarcely in position when they heard footsteps coming down the ladder from just below the hatch opening.

Aiko held the pillow lengthwise so it covered her torso, but still low enough so the man could get a glimpse of her cleavage. She felt her heartbeat increasing, but controlled her breathing, giving her a mental and emotional advantage.

"Please, don't stop on my account," the man chuckled.

The cuts and bruises from the recent fight were easily seen even in the scant tunnel light.

"Hey Mister, you were told not to hit the girls in the face. That is going to cost you extra," Masato's man said sternly. He started to take a step closer to the couple, a gesture that caused Oksana to shrink farther under the bed.

There was little light under the bed, but Oksana could see a large hole in the underside of the mattress.

Inside the hole, a pair of little red beady eyes stared back at her. The rat shuffled forward and stuck his head out of the hole, causing Oksana to flinch.

Oksana's movement caught the man's attention and just as he turned toward the bed, a muffled sound came through the pillow causing very little echo within the small tunnel space. Masato's man hit the ground, dead. Aiko had used Kyle's gun to put two rounds into the man, using the pillow as a silencer. The burn marks that erupted through the pillow were still smoking like a volcanic explosion. Feathers erupted like lava, making two small craters in the back of the pillow. A few of those feathers danced in the air, riding what little draft there was coming down the hatch from the warehouse.

Chapter 27

Oksana stayed under the bed while Kyle and Aiko put their clothes back on. Masato's man laid dead, his lifeless eyes staring at her.

"It's okay to come out, Oksana."

Cautiously the frightened teenager crawled out from under the bed, her eyes trying to avoid contact with the dead man on the ground. She handed the sword back to Aiko.

Aiko's smile was barely noticeable as Kyle gently removed a couple of large down feathers from Oksana's hair.

"There's a large rat under the bed," Oksana said, fear in her voice.

"Did he bite you?" Kyle asked, his eyes quickly scanning over Oksana, checking for any injuries.

"No."

"Then maybe it was just as scared of you, as you were of it."

"Maybe."

Kyle put his arm around her shoulders, trying to reassure her.

"This way, Oksana," Aiko said as she walked to the stairs.

She watched Oksana tuck her long black and white robe under its belt so she could climb the old staircase easier.

While Aiko and Oksana ascended the stairs, Kyle searched the dead man for any weapons that might come in handy. He found a set of keys and a swipe card and put them in his pocket. He then shoved the body under the bed, delaying any immediate red flags should someone else be checking the tunnel. By the time Kyle reached the top of the stairs, the girls were gone. Following two sets of dirty footprints, he turned a corner just as they were going up the steps leading to the catwalk in front of Masato's office. He caught up with them as they were ready to enter the office.

"Please, Kyle," Aiko asked. "Wait here and keep watch. Knock twice lightly if you see anyone."

Aiko opened the office door and guided Oksana through it with a gentle hand. "Come with me, Oksana." The girls went into the office and closed the door.

Inside, Aiko led Oksana to a closet. The closet contained the most beautiful clothes Oksana had ever seen. She admired the soft silks in their rich colors. Her fingers desperately wanted to touch the textures.

Afraid of leaving a mark on the exquisite clothing, she put her hands under her armpits to keep from reaching out for them.

Most females would have been envious of the wardrobe, but for Aiko, it represented a lifetime of servitude. This is why when she started to untie the knots of Kyle's white dress shirt, she stopped. At that moment Aiko realized, not only did she not have to put on any of the clothes in the closet, but she preferred the clothes Kyle had given her, especially his shirt. Guiding Oksana to the closet, she told her to pick out something to wear, anything she wanted. As Oksana fretted over what to choose, Aiko grabbed a brush, combed through her own hair, and put it in a ponytail.

After Oksana had dressed, she asked to borrow the hair brush. Aiko surprised Oksana again when she fastened a beautiful jade comb in her hair.

"This comb is for you."

"Thank you."

Satisfied with their appearance, Aiko told Oksana to follow her to Masato's office. On a bookshelf near Masato's desk, sat the Guardian on its stand.

"Let me show you something, Oksana." She pointed to the ancient sword and the one-of-a-kind presentation stand it sat on. "The sword master who made this katana also made this stand. His name was Kaji. There was to be a set of swords presented to Masato's ancestral grandfather, but the sword master died before completing the katana. Legend has it that he did manage to complete the tanto."

"What is a tanto?"

"It is a smaller version of this katana, complete with precious gemstones that make it one-of-a-kind."

"Where is it?"

"It is here. This word here tells us its location."

Aiko pointed to the writing on the side of the stand. Oksana's eyes, wide with curiosity, gazed at the writing and elaborate etchings.

"What does it say?"

"This is written in an old Japanese language called, Kojiki. And this word here means, the Guardian. And these two symbols—"

"Yin and Yang."

"That's right. Notice the black half is above the white."

"What does that mean?"

"One of the meanings for yin, represented by the dark half of the symbol, is downward. And for yang, the white means upward."

Oksana paused and studied the symbols before speaking. "So, they are reversed?"

"Yes."

Aiko and Oksana each grabbed a symbol and turned it outwardly as a dial, reversing the polarity of the symbol. The face at the base of the stand was actually the face of a drawer and was spring loaded. As they reached the desired positions, the yang on top and yin below, the drawer sprung open. Aiko pulled the drawer the rest of the way open. She reached inside and pulled out an object wrapped in a red silk cloth.

"Hold out your hands, Oksana." The girl obeyed and Aiko placed the object in her hands. After it was unwrapped, Aiko said in a reverent tone of voice, "This has belonged in Masato's family for hundreds of years. It is known as a tanto."

The tanto in its scabbard was about twenty-two inches in length, with an eleven inch, razor-sharp blade and a seven inch intricately hand-carved, bone-white, ivory handle. It was art personified and contained all four precious stones. The ivory handle came from Africa along an old trade route known as the Silk Route to Japan.

Carved into the end of the handle was the head of a tiger, with its mouth open, as if it was roaring. Also from Africa, were two brilliant one-carat diamonds for the eyes. A three-carat blood red ruby for a tongue came from Thailand. Near the hilt on each side of the handle, were the symbols for yin and yang. These were made from matching descending swirls of dark green emeralds from Cambodia and light-colored sapphires from Sri Lanka. The largest of the four emerald stones was two carats, each descending stone dropped down a half-carat in size. It was the same pattern for the matching sapphires mounted in a 24-carat gold facet. This made the tanto a one-of-a-kind, flawless and priceless masterpiece.

Kyle was on the catwalk, listening to the faint sounds of traffic outside the warehouse. As he waited for the girls, he noticed the catwalk was still tarnished from Aiko's dried blood. He realized then how much had transpired in the last few days. Looking beyond the stain to the floor below, images of holding his brother as he died came rushing over him like a massive emotional tidal wave. All of the events that led up to this moment had overwhelmed him and yet gave him such direction at the same time. He reflected on something his mother had once told him. *"When it comes to love, our heart doesn't always tell us why we fall in love, we just do."*

A cell phone on Masato's desk pinged. Aiko and Oksana also notice there was a laptop open but the screen was dark. Oksana tapped the pad and the screen reactivated. Masato was in such a hurry he had left his email open but it was asking for a password.

"Let's go, Oksana. We need to leave."

"I can get in."

"What?"

"I think I can get in. That is, if you want me to?"

"How?"

"Do you know the phone number to this phone?"

"He has more than one cell phone. I do not know the numbers for all of them."

Oksana pulled open the top right-hand drawer and fumbled through it.

"What are you looking for Oksana?"

"An invoice."

Aiko opened a cabinet drawer and pulled out a shipping invoice. "Here's one."

"Is there a contact number?"

"Yes."

Oksana moved the cursor to the top right corner of the email screen and signed out. Then she clicked on the "Sign in" button. It immediately asked for a password. Oksana slid the cursor to the "Can't access your account" button. The prompt asked, "Please enter your phone number to get a text with a new temporary password."

Oksana entered the phone number but just before she sent it, Aiko stopped her. "What if this is the wrong phone?"

"I don't see an office phone so this should be the one. Only one way to find out."

Aiko nodded and Oksana sent the number.

There was a long pause but then the phone *pinged*. Oksana checked the text and had the new password. She entered it. Oksana dropped the email page down and a moment later, they were both looking at the screen's desktop.

There were about twenty files on the screen but there were only a few that stood out for Aiko. They were files labeled: Aiko, Assets, Company Holdings, and Morrell.

"Click on the one that says, Morrell."

The file opened and had a series of sub-files: Capt. Morrell, Lydia, Kyle, and Steven.

Aiko was without words and pointed to the file marked, Lydia.

Oksana opened the file and they saw a full history going back for years.

"Try the one marked, Assets."

Oksana opened the file. Again, more sub-files marked: Bids, Location, and Vendors.

Aiko requested, "Bids."

A photo popped up of a young woman about sixteen years old with a price under her name of $7,000. What shocked Aiko the most, was off to the left it said, 1 of 327 and the "NEXT" button was lit up. Oksana began to click it over and over. Up came a file and image of another girl, then another, one after another.

"Stop, Oksana."

Oksana went back to the sub-file.

Aiko was afraid to look but asked, "Location?"

The cursor slowly slid down and stopped on the heading. Click.

A map of the world appeared and it was lit up with hundreds of red dots. Oksana zoomed in on South America, then closer on Brazil and even closer until the dots on the screen were separated. She clicked on one of the dots and a bio of a client known as a Vendor and his purchased asset appeared, along with her picture. Blonde, blue eyes, and scared as hell.

"Oksana, how do we save this?"

Oksana went back to the top desk drawer and pulled out a flash drive she had seen there earlier and held it up to show Aiko.

Out on the catwalk, Kyle was wondering what was taking so long and was getting anxious. A minute later, the door to Masato's office opened and the girls stepped out. Oksana wore one of Aiko's white karate gi uniforms, tied closed around the waist by a black belt.

"Find what you were looking for?" Kyle asked.

Aiko showed Kyle the Guardian.

"What? You didn't like the one I gave you?" Kyle said with a smirk.

"Yes, enough to pass it on."

"What is that supposed to mean?"

"If it was worthless, why would I want to give to anyone else?"

The large loading dock doors to the bay began to open.

"This way," Aiko insisted. She led them across the catwalk to another set of stairs going up, and in the opposite direction from Masato's office.

Just as they disappeared from view, Masato's car entered the bay.

Chapter 28

Heavy layers of insulation covered the windows in the massive room where the various sets of sexual escapades continued to play out. While the girls were forced to carry out explicit fantasies for their paying clientele, it didn't matter what time of day it was or what was happening outside the confines of the building. The insulation didn't allow noise or light from the outside in, and it kept any noise inside from filtering out.

One female, posing as a college student in her dorm room, appeared to have just returned from a jog. She slowly stripped out of her sweat suit and tossed it onto the bed, disturbing the cat, causing it to jump off and run away. Slowly, she took off her jogging bra and matching panties, teasing her client on the other end of the pay-per-view. Another girl acted out the role of a secretary. She had just let her hair down, removed her glasses and was beginning to undo her blouse when a young man acting like her boss, walked up behind her and started helping her undress.

The set, designed to look like a high school girl's locker room had two girls dressed as cheerleaders and a guy in the role of the jock.

During the production, a small team of captive guys and girls took turns in sexual role-playing, while the camera crew filmed what would become a low-budget production for DVD sales.

Erica, Masato's latest project, was an enticing young woman in her early twenties, who showed much more promise than his other girls. Her long strawberry-blonde hair and deep blue eyes made her a natural for the business. Masato had bargained for her as part of the deal between him and Pankov when they merged.

"Throw in that tasteful morsel and you've got a deal," he had told Pankov. The deal would have gone through anyway, he just wanted her for himself. Masato had taken his time with her. He had given her special attention and rewarded her well. He wanted her on display so he could enjoy her physical assets. This is why he made Erica his head of production. She sat at the central control center, emotionless. That part of her life had been removed for all intents and purposes. When Masato first saw her, he knew she was different, one not easily broken down and turned into someone else's prized possession of affection. She had a will of her own. With the right guidance, he could sculpt her like he did Aiko. He gave her the chance to work with him or for him.

Soon she was no longer in front of the camera but behind it running the show. It was a way of showing the girls they too might have a way out. Erica knew there was no way out so she had given in, hoping to make the best of it, and that included a percentage of the sales. There were days like today when she found herself looking past the monitors at the girls. They were all playing out fantasies for the clients and she found herself without empathy or remorse, frozen in time and without…emotion. That was the price she had to pay to not be sold.

Suddenly, the cat jumped onto her console and knocked over the cup of hot tea she was drinking. She grabbed the cat and tossed it onto the floor, shooing it away with her foot.

*****

Having personal knowledge of the building layout, Aiko led Kyle and Oksana away from the activity to a quiet corner of the floor where a new, empty set was under construction. This set was a patio with a hot tub, complete with latticework, covered in fake ivy to help create the outdoor look. The three of them sat down, exhausted, thirsty and hungry.

Quietly Kyle said, "It looks like the only way out is back down the stairs, unless you know of another option?"

Aiko, sitting near a window covered with insulation, stood up and peeled back a corner of the insulation. She peered out the window and saw a dumpster area, fully lit as it sat directly underneath a street light below them. A few rubber 55-gallon barrels with chains were linked together, with the bottoms of the barrels removed. They formed a tube from a large window not far from them to a dumpster below. The tube was used by workers for debris that needed to be disposed of from their floor to the dumpsters below.

"Maybe," Aiko muttered softly.

She felt Kyle standing behind her, looking at the string of barrels. "Are you serious?"

Irritated over his skepticism of her plan, Aiko gave Kyle a look that made him decidedly uncomfortable. She motioned to him and Oksana to follow her to the large window where the barrels were tied together. The two adults carefully opened the window with as little noise as possible. Kyle started to empty small boxes that were filled with four one-gallon plastic bottles of pool acid. He set the plastic bottles aside, folded the boxes closed, and threw the empty cardboard boxes down the chute. Grabbing any insulation, she could find, Aiko used the katana and cut the insulation into strips then sent it down the barrels.

*****

Before opening the door to his office, Masato stood on the catwalk giving orders to his men.

"Make sure this place is locked up tight and check on the girls."

"Yes, Master," replied one of the men.

The second Masato opened his office door, he knew somebody had recently been in there. Aromas still lingered in the air, one of them especially familiar to his nose, Aiko. What he noticed next was the missing Guardian sword, and in its place, a sword of inferior quality. He pulled it from the stand and drew it from its scabbard.

"Amateurs," Masato said with disgust.

He then checked the other room. On the floor was Oksana's black and white robe. Masato hurried out of the office and screamed to his men, "There are intruders in this building, find them!"

Returning to his office, Masato called Erica at the control center. "There are trespassers in the building. Notify me immediately if you hear or see anything. And shut down the sets."

"Yes, master sensei," Erica answered. From

the master control panel, she turned off the lights and other electronic equipment on the set. Her next step was to instruct the indentured talent to leave their positions and go to the elevators. Once everyone was gathered by the elevators, Erica used her electronic swipe card to release the elevator doors and let them inside. The elevator was sent up. Its doors opened and a guard was there to escort them to their dorm rooms, located on the top floor.

Meanwhile, Erica had turned her focus to the dimly lit room to listen for any noise and to watch for any movement that might indicate outsiders were present.

After an undetermined amount of time, the distant sound of a boat horn was heard coming from a nearby dock. The noise made Erica take notice. It had filtered through what should have been enough insulation to mute the sound. She strained to listen for anything else out of the ordinary. Then she heard it, a sound like lead pipes banging together. Erica called Masato on the phone. "They're here." After a pause, she said, "Yes, I understand."

Kyle had accidentally kicked a small stack of lead pipes lying on the floor. He carefully rested his foot on them to keep them from clanging again.

After a minute, he slowly lifted his foot away and waited to hear if anyone had noticed.

Erica cautiously made her way to the only stairwell leading to the ground floor. As she removed her pistol from her shoulder harness, she checked the clip and sent it home with a loud click, to let the intruders know she was armed. In a confident, firm voice she said, "There's nowhere to go."

From where Erica stood near the stairwell, she couldn't see around to the backside of the hot tub set where Aiko and Kyle were. The couple continued to load more insulation down the barrel chute, unaware Erica could hear the faint whispers of their conversation.

The threesome knew they didn't have much time.

"Well, she knows we're here, so this shouldn't matter," Kyle said as he frantically yanked down a long piece of insulation from the window. Light from the streetlamp burst into the room. Aiko trimmed it down into smaller sizes with the katana as fast as she could, then shoved it down the chute. Once they exhausted all their options for a soft landing at the bottom of the chute, they found a 25-foot orange extension cord that was plugged into the hot tub. They used it as a rope, tying off one end to a nearby post. Taking the other end, Aiko tossed it down the string of barrels that led to the dumpster.

"Okay, Oksana," Kyle whispered. "Once you get inside the barrels, I want you to wrap the cord around your leg, and where it crosses over your foot, step on it with your other foot. This is how you can control your speed going down, by stepping on the cord."

Aiko gave Oksana a reassuring look before she and Kyle helped her climb into the chute and prepare to slide down. A shaky Oksana wrapped the cord around her leg and stepped on it like Kyle instructed.

"That's it, you're doing great, Oksana," Kyle encouraged.

The teenager slowly made her way down. Her frightened brown eyes flickered back and forth between the couple above her and whatever waited for her below.

Aiko spoke softly in Kyle's ear. "The cord, it is not long enough."

"I know," Kyle replied in the same soft tone. He turned his attention back to Oksana. "We'll be right behind you."

"No, you won't," Masato's voice boomed.

The sound of Masato's voice startled Oksana as it reverberated down the barrel chute and she lost her grip on the extension cord. She slid down fifteen feet, stopping short oft the end of the cord. The cord was now stretched to its limit and the knot tied around the post was slipping. Only the large end of the three-pronged socket kept the entire knot from coming untied. Oksana was stopped half-way down the length of the barrels. She looked up the chute, then down, unable to let go of the cord. She could feel the other end of the cord's receptacle between her feet.

Aiko raised her sword to cut the extension cord, hoping to help Oksana get away. Just as she raised the sword, Erica shot her, grazing her shoulder. The action caused Aiko to spin and fall backward, missing the cord when her arm came down.

Kyle rushed to her side. "Are you alright?" His hands gingerly touched around her wound. Aiko nodded, then turned her attention to her father. The look she gave him was one of pure hatred.

"She's your daughter!" Kyle shouted to Masato.

"I have many daughters." Masato glared at Aiko as a smile formed at the corners of his mouth.

He held the sword Aiko had left in his office in his right hand.

This was the first time Aiko heard Masato openly admit she was his daughter. The rage she felt for him intensified and became mixed with shame. She pushed Kyle's hands away, as well as, the pain searing through her body. With one lithe movement, she was on her feet, her sword pointed at her father in challenge form.

Erica pointed her gun at Aiko for the second time, ready to take a shot.

"Stop," Masato commanded as he put his hand on Erica's gun. Never taking his eyes off Aiko, he took the gun from Erica and replaced it with the replica sword Kyle had bought for Aiko. "Now, it is an even fight," he said.

Erica's grin was spiteful as she approached Aiko, sizing her up for the easy defeat she believed was inevitable. Aiko stared into Erica's cold blue eyes as she moved slowly and methodically to counter her movements, like an endangered animal stalking its prey.

"May your eternal sleep be a peaceful one, Aiko," Erica hissed as she stepped forward and swung her sword at the wounded exotic samurai.

Chapter 29

The frustration of being unable to help Aiko chewed at Kyle as he watched the sparring of Masato's feline subjects engage in an intense, yet efficient sword fight for dominance. Masato stood at the top of the stairs blocking the exit, his gun pointed aimlessly in Kyle's direction. With every reverberating sound of the steel blades clashing, the detective's fury increased. He could neither participate in Aiko's fight nor check to see what happened, if anything, to Oksana.

Erica tested her counterpart's abilities, to see just how far she was willing to go. They moved like two wild exotic cats from the same jungle. Aiko was like a tiger, willing to use her stealth and patience to stalk her prey. Erica's impersonation emulated a jaguar, relying on strength and speed for the kill.

The claws came out, and after several clashes, Erica noticed her blade was not holding up to the quality of her opponent's katana. She realized she could not continue to play this way with Aiko. With a quick thrust and a flick of her wrist, Erica's blade put a small slice in Aiko's right forearm. In the same motion, as she passed by her, Erica threw her elbow into Aiko's shoulder wound. Immediately the blood flowed again. The small stream of blood was staining the white shirt Kyle had given Aiko to wear as a temporary tourniquet.

Aiko was losing the feeling and strength in her right hand, which she needed to hold the sword properly, so she quickly switched it to her left hand. This sign of weakness did not go unnoticed by Erica. She threw a kick into Aiko's right side, forcing her to block it with her right arm. The full contact was enough to tear the stitches loose from the front side of her through and through. As the blood flowed, it formed a pattern like a crimson rose, blooming in fast forward. Aiko played up the pain, drawing Erica in closer to her. Dropping to one knee, Aiko did a swift pirouette, letting her momentum aid in the power as she brought her blade around, catching Erica across the side of her knee. The damage wasn't as crippling to Erica as Aiko would have liked, but it was enough to get her attention.

For the first time, Erica broke out in a full sweat from the physical pain. She started to wonder, "Who's toying with whom?"

Erica pounced, and in a series of fluid strikes with her sword, she added more shallow cuts to Aiko's already tattered and worn body.

The tenacious five-minute attack by Erica felt like fifteen minutes of torture for Aiko. Knowing she had the strength for only one more charge, Aiko decided her best offense would be a counter move. She waited while Erica used the back of her wrist to wipe away blood and sweat from her brow. The piercing eyes of Erica never left Aiko's face as she licked the bodily fluids off her wrist. She smiled as she said, "The good news is, it's not mine."

Both women then moved in opposing arcs. With each crossover step, Aiko made with her right foot, she winced in pain. Kyle and Erica both observed the expression on Aiko's face. Kyle could do nothing, but Erica poised herself like a cobra, ready to strike. She nodded at Aiko before she raised her sword and stepped in with an all-in-one move. In an effort to defend herself, Aiko raised her sword up. The pain in her arm was debilitating, causing a slow reflex. She did manage to block Erica's initial thrust, but not enough to avoid the full contact of Erica's fist to the side of her ribs. For Aiko, that blow felt like her right side had collapsed and she gasped for air. By now, her back was to the windows and with a final effort, she raised her sword with both hands.

This left her body open and a front kick from Erica knocked Aiko against a pillar next to the open window. Her right shoulder slammed into the pillar, the searing pain in her shoulder caused her to lose her grip on the Guardian. The katana flew out of her hand and in the direction of the open window.

Aiko's adrenaline kicked in and she screamed, "Oksana!"

As Aiko whirled, she was unable to reach the katana in time to grab it out of the air. All she could do was slap it up against the inside of the first barrel. When it finally came to rest, it was held in place by two of Aiko's fingertips. She knew she could not risk trying to re-grip the handle.

"Oksana, you have to let go, I can't hold this!" Aiko yelled.

Aiko's voice startled the frightened girl and she let go of the cord. Before she had time to breathe, she was lying on top of the insulation in the dumpster. The Guardian slipped from Aiko's fingers and banged on the side of the barrel with a loud clang. A noise at the top of the barrel tube inspired Oksana to roll to the side just before the Guardian landed tip down, piercing deep into the insulation.

Unnerved, she lay perfectly still while trying to control her heavy breathing, the sword was less than two feet from her head.

From deep within, Aiko found the strength to run to the window just as the sword landed in the dumpster. Peering out the window, she saw Oksana's scared face looking up at her. Seeing she was unharmed, Aiko turned back toward her opponent.

Oksana grabbed the Guardian and tossed it outside the dumpster. She heard it clatter as it hit the ground. When she climbed out of the dumpster, the sword was not on the ground, it was in the hands of Captain Morrell.

The recent loss of Steven and internal conflicts showed heavily on the Captain. His unkempt appearance frightened the young girl. Panic projected from Oksana's eyes and she gasped.

"Don't be afraid, I'm here to help you," Morrell said, his voice a mixture of softness and sadness.

Before Oksana could speak, Hitoshi pistol-whipped Morrell from behind causing him to drop to one knee. The sword fell out of his hand.

"Run," he managed to spit out before being grabbed by the collar and pushed up against the dumpster.

Oksana turned and fled around the side of the dumpster. She didn't get very far before her escape route was cut off by a stack of debris and other supplies for the new construction.

Hitoshi laughed, "She won't get far."

"You know, your boss isn't going to like the fact you let a little girl get away from you," Morrell said in an uneven tone of voice.

*****

"Kyle," Aiko's voice was filled with concern and solace.

Kyle went to the window where Aiko stood. Looking over her shoulder, he saw his father being confronted by Hitoshi. The look on Hitoshi's face showed a venomous rage. e took the Guardian, spun Morrell around, and pushed him up against the dumpster, running the sword through his midsection. The blade passed through Morrell's body with ease and stopped only when the tip of the blade hit the side of the dumpster with the dull ping.

"No!" Kyle's anger bellowed out of him from deep within.

He watched in horror as Hitoshi slid the blade back and forth effortlessly like a violin bow through his father. With each stroke he heard a tap, tap, tap against the dumpster.

"Kyle, I am sorry, but there is nothing we can do for him. We need to focus," pleaded Aiko.

Erica and Masato watched with amusement the emotional turmoil on Kyle's face. Masato caressed Erica's back, a hint of their emotional connection to each other. He leaned into her and smelled the heat of her sweating skin. It pleased him as much as the aroma from a fine bottle of red wine and the remnants of their moments of passion.

Kyle stepped out from behind the hot tub set holding a four-foot steel pipe in his hand. Masato smiled at Kyle's attempt at chivalry.

There was no forethought in Kyle's actions. It didn't occur to him to stop and consider what he was going up against. He raised the pipe like a baseball bat and drew it back as if to take a home run swing. He didn't realize he had left himself wide open. Erica took one step forward and with a roundhouse kick, caught Kyle squarely in the chest with her heel, knocking him backward. He knew then, he would need to reassess his situation.

The pipe he was holding was about a foot longer than Erica's katana. There was something else Kyle noticed, Erica's stance revealed that she was right-handed, the same as him. Leading with his right foot, he positioned himself in the same stance as Erica. He remembered his experiences with Aiko on the houseboat and how he had made the mistake of giving her the cue that he was ready to begin. Aiko had told him, "If you only have one second to make a decision, you may have just wasted it."

Erica taunted him by reaching out and flicking the end of the blade against Kyle's makeshift weapon of choice. As she drew it back, Kyle lunged and Erica countered, but not before taking a solid hit to her shoulder from the end of the pipe. It squarely connected, but Erica's skills were still too advanced for Kyle. The hit to her shoulder spun her around and left her back to Kyle. She thrust her left elbow into his gut and as Kyle bent over from the blow, Erica brought up her fist and gave him a hard backhand punch to the face. Kyle's knees buckled. Lowering her center of gravity, Erica swept her left leg around, catching Kyle off guard. It was a low contact across the back of his feet, sweeping them out from under him. The action landed Kyle flat on his back.

The next few seconds were a blur. Pain found every part of his body. He caught the shimmer of the light coming through the window from the street lamp, reflecting off Erica's blade as it was coming down. With the end of the pipe still in his right hand, he brought it across his face catching the other end in his left hand, turning his head away as Erica's blade made contact. *SNAP*! The blade of the cheap replica katana Erica was now using broke in half as it struck the pipe. The top half rotated down and entered into Kyle's shoulder like a dagger.

Searing hot pain shot through every nerve in his shoulder like an out of control wildfire. Erica was about to plunge the other half of the sword into Kyle when Aiko, with a steel pipe of her own, blocked the downward swing. Kyle looked up and saw Aiko's foot make full contact to Erica's ribs. It knocked Erica back onto the floor. With cat-like reflexes, Erica rolled and sprang back to her feet. She flashed a wicked grin at the battered and bleeding couple. Despite her gains in the battle, she needed a moment to catch her own breath and tend to the cut on the side of her knee. She removed her designer leather belt, wrapped it tightly around her leg just above her knee and locked the clasp in place to slow the bleeding.

When she was done, Erica focused her attention on watching the interaction between Aiko and Kyle.

Without warning, Aiko grabbed the blade in Kyle's shoulder and yanked it out.

"Ahhhh!" Kyle screamed. He took a deep breath before berating Aiko. "What happened to, one-two-three?"

"Three," Aiko said as she ripped off her other sleeve and wrapped it under his arm and over his shoulder, tying it off as tight as she could to stop the bleeding.

Energized by her anger, Aiko took Kyle's pipe and tossed it toward Erica. The pipe rolled and clanged across the floor until it was stopped when Erica stepped on it.

Chapter 30

Captain Morrell managed to stand upright and lean against the dumpster, despite Hitoshi's tight grip on the Guardian.

His voice barely above a whisper, Morrell asked, "What now?"

"A lesson in craftsmanship, Captain. Did you notice how the blade passed right through you, as you American's say, "Just like butter?" All I have to do is pull it to the side and I will open you right up like a slaughtered pig."

Captain Morrell coughed up blood. Every minor movement he made sent jolts of excruciating pain through his body. The darkness of unconsciousness descended upon him in waves.

"Don't die on me yet, Captain. Once I remove the blade, you will have about thirty seconds to decide what your life is worth."

"I already know," Morrell groaned.

Hitoshi leaned into the dying officer and whispered, "It doesn't matter. You have outlived your usefulness."

With the last of his strength, Morrell head-butted his killer and sent him stumbling back against another dumpster.

He spun around and leaned back with all his weight into Hitoshi, pinning him against the side of the dumpster. Morrell grabbed the sword handle and shoved it the rest of the way through his body and into Hitoshi's mid-section. He then firmly gripped the sword handle and turned his body, pivoting, and slicing through Hitoshi's midsection. This created an act similar to seppuku, the samurai bushido honor of the Japanese suicide ritual, known as hara-kiri. After taking a few steps forward, Morrell turned and watched as Hitoshi's dead, disemboweled body hit the ground.

Despite his labored breathing, Morrell heard a soft cry nearby. He turned to see Oksana staring at him. Smiling weakly and with a dry mouth, he said to her, "Just like butter."

The sound of pipes clashing and clanging somewhere above them diverted Oksana's and Morrell's attention toward the noise.

*****

The battle between Aiko and Erica was now at full throttle. After every few strikes of their pipes, the enemies paused to study each other. During the fight, Aiko caught another glimpse of the tattoo at the small of Erica's back.

The extreme fighting had reached a stalemate. Aiko concluded that the only way to end the fight was by hand-to-hand combat. She threw her pipe to the ground, daring Erica to do the same. Gladly accepting the challenge, Erica glared at Aiko as she tossed her pipe to the floor.

As soon as the pipes hit the floor, it was as if the bell rang on the last round in a prize fight. Erica pounced, catching Aiko with a front kick to the midsection. It sent Aiko backwards, her head hitting hard enough against the window to crack the glass. The impression it left in the shattered window looked a lot like the shape of a fractured spider web. A large spot of Aiko's blood from her scalp resembled a large spider in the center of it. Aiko turned her head enough to catch a glimpse of the scene below. Hitoshi was dead on the ground, Oksana was looking at her, fear frozen on her face, and the handle of the Guardian was protruding from Captain Morrell's mid-section.

What needed to be done next took no second thought by Morrell. He walked to the ladder that was welded to the side of the dumpster, pulled the sword from his body and with only thirty seconds left to live, managed to climb the metal ladder.

With the greatest of difficulty, Morrell moved close enough to the barrel chute that emptied into the dumpster and shoved the Guardian, blade up, through the bottom of the second to the last barrel. The tip of the blade barely made it through the other side, but it was enough to hold it firmly in its place. It was a father's last gesture to try to regain his honor in front of his son. Morrell's body slumped from the ladder to the ground. Oksana knelt by his side, putting her ear close to Morrell's lips to hear his dying words.

"Tell Kyle, I love . . ."

*****

Aiko turned her attention to Erica, determined more than ever to defeat her new rival. It was time to take control of the fight, and her destiny. Since both women had the same additional training from Masato, they were equally skilled in the disciplines of karate and jujitsu. It was going to take more than just knowledge of the arts to defeat one another. It was going to take a desire from deep within one's heart, mind, and soul to find victory.

A kick from Aiko to the inside of Erica's knee and an elbow firmly jabbed to the back of her neck, caused Erica to fall face down, hard to the floor.

While she was temporarily winded, Aiko jumped on her back, gripped the back of her black blouse and ripped it open. Erica's Jaguar tattoo stared back at her. It covered her back in the same location and manner as her own black and white tiger stripes. The bright yellows and the warm browns painted a background for a unique pattern of individual black patches that made up the mesmerizing tattoo. It was astonishing for Aiko to see another woman adorned like her. She thought, *"How many more like her? Like us?"*

Aiko's distraction cost her. Erica whirled and threw her off. The fight for survival was back on. After several strikes were delivered and more blood was drawn by both women, Erica finally got a scissor kick into Aiko's midsection. It sent her back a few feet, in front of the open window. With her back to the window, Aiko challenged Erica with a loud scream. Enraged by her refusal to give up, Erica reacted by charging Aiko, her aggressive nature momentarily blinded her to Aiko's maneuvers. Using Erica's own forward momentum against her, Aiko grabbed her and rolled herself back onto the floor. Using her legs, Aiko sent Erica flying through the open window. She entered the chute with enough force that she couldn't stop herself from going in.

Her natural reaction was to throw her arms and legs out to the sides of the barrel to slow her descent, it worked. Seeing the power cord, Erica grabbed it with one hand and then the other and hung on. After sliding halfway down the cord, she finally was able to stop her momentum. Kyle and Aiko could see the cord go taut. Erica got her feet under her and kicked off one shoe at a time for better traction. One shoe passed by the blade at the bottom of the chute, the other sliced in two without hesitation. Erica began to scale back up the chute.

Kyle looked down the barrels and could see Erica's arrogant look of, "Nice try."

He turned and kicked the already strained knot of the power cord that was lashed around the post at their end. The tension was too much for it to release.

During this intense physical battle, the stray cat was just a few feet away, watching. Kyle picked it up and tossed it down the chute.

Erica's screams echoed within the barrels until they abruptly stopped when she was sliced in half by the Guardian poised at the bottom of the chute. Oksana stood not far from the dumpster, Erica's screams reverberating in her mind. When Erica's body parts landed in the dumpster, Oksana buried her face in her hands and sobbed.

Suddenly, the cat sprang from the dumpster, startling the crying girl. She looked up to see it running away, with only a part of its tail missing.

Chapter 31

Tired and drained of all emotions, Oksana remembered what Aiko had said, the Guardian was the key. Oksana climbed up the ladder on the side of the dumpster. She reached up and retrieved the katana, pulling it out from the plastic barrel. The climb back down was not as difficult as trying to avoid a view of Erica's dead body, lying in pieces in the dumpster.

Aiko stared at Masato's gun only inches from her face.

"You can come out now, Detective Morrell. Its negotiation time," Masato said snidely. His cool, in-control facade was starting to show small lines of cracking. "One of you is going to tell me where the tanto is or the other one of you will die."

Kyle was leaning against the hot tub when Masato summoned him. He walked over and stood next to Aiko, they exchanged brief glances of concern for one another.

Masato pointed his gun at Kyle's head, the sound of the slide echoed loudly as he racked it back.

"I know where it is," Aiko said.

"So, you are willing to trade your life for his," Masato said with contempt.

A look of mutual understanding passed between Kyle and Aiko.

"Aiko, you know you don't have to do this," Kyle said.

"You should be honored detective, to have someone who is of such stature as Aiko, willing to die for you."

*****

In Masato's office, beams of light from the morning sun's rays shimmered through the window highlighting the sword stand, casting shadows across the raised letters that accentuated the ancient text.

Staring at the symbols in the kojiki text, Masato asked, "Does it tell us where the tanto is hidden?"

Forced to their knees, Kyle and Aiko were side by side, only a few feet in front of Masato.

"It says. . . The Guardian," Aiko replied.

"Meaning what?"

"It's about honor, to watch over someone else's life, to protect."

Masato was finding it nearly impossible to control his anger. He glared at the two lovers as he said, "What are you implying, Aiko?"

Before Aiko could respond, Kyle interrupted, "There is no tanto, no ancient masterpiece. It was only meant as some sort of code to live by."

"And you know this how, detective? Because she told you?" Masato glanced at Aiko.

Kyle was about to speak when Masato interrupted him. "If what you just said is true, then I no longer need either of you." He pointed his gun at Aiko's head.

"Stop!" Kyle yelled, "She's your daughter. Doesn't that mean anything to you?"

"I gave her a life filled with the highest education and training and what does she do? She betrays me." Masato raised his voice to a level Aiko had never heard before. "She betrayed me!"

"What you did was make her your concubine. What kind of life was that?"

"Aaaaah!" Masato screamed as he hit the side of Kyle's head with his gun.

"No!" Aiko wept as she reached to hold Kyle.

"Take a good look at her, detective," Masato mocked. "She is useless to me or to anybody else. No one will want her now, she cannot even bear children."

"I want her," Kyle said.

Aiko's tears were for a different reason now as she listened to Kyle's confession. "Aiko is beautiful, strong and loyal."

"So, you are willing to die for her?"

"Yes, I am," said Kyle.

Movement at the office doorway caught the attention of Masato, Kyle and Aiko. It was Oksana, watching the drama unfold, the Guardian in her hand.

"Then you might just get your chance," said Masato.

He motioned with his hand for Oksana to come in. He ordered, "Bring it here, my little one."

Oksana didn't move.

"I said bring it to me now, Oksana!" Masato shouted. Oksana obeyed and walked across the room to hand him the sword.

"I am going to teach you to be as strong and special as your Aiko here," Masato said as he pushed the girl behind him. She fell, hitting hard against the back shelf in front of the sword stand.

Masato turned the sword over at different angles so blinding glints of light hit Kyle and Aiko across their eyes. "Tell me, detective, what should I believe, the legend or your lies? One thing is for sure. At least the legend will live on."

"What if I know where it is?" Oksana said, her speech hurried and shaky.

"No, Oksana," Aiko begged.

Oksana got to her feet. "What if I can tell you where it is? Will you let them go?"

"You can't trust him, Oksana," Kyle insisted.

"Quiet!" shouted Masato. He rested the end of the Guardian on Aiko's shoulder, the razor-sharp blade close to her neck. "Go on, Oksana, what are you trying to say? Did Aiko tell you where it is hidden?"

Oksana saw the pain in Aiko's eyes.

"She told me how special it is and—"

"Oksana, you don't want—" Before she could finish her sentence, Masato pressed the edge of the blade to the side of Aiko's neck. The slight movement drew blood.

Terrified for Aiko, Oksana quickly continued, "I will tell you what she told me about the tanto."

The mere mention of the tanto captured Masato's full attention.

Oksana continued, "Aiko told me that the man who made this stand also made . . ."

"Yes, go on," Masato insisted.

Oksana ignored Kyle as he shook his head and kept talking. "Aiko said, he died before he could complete the swords for your ancestor."

Masato was enraged.

"Is that true?" asked Oksana.

In response to her question, Masato backhanded the child.

Aiko shouted at Masato, "She is telling the truth!"

Becoming angrier by the minute, Masato turned his back on Oksana to deal with Kyle and Aiko. "I have heard enough of these lies!"

From the corner of his eye, Kyle saw Oksana reach out to the sword stand with both hands. He raised his voice to keep Masato's attention away from her.

"You said it yourself, it's about honor. He was making the swords to honor your ancestors. Is this the way you want to be remembered?"

"I don't need some gaijin to tell me about honor," Masato hissed.

The couple watched in horror as Masato raised the sword high above his head, ready to come down on Kyle in one powerful swing. Just as Masato's grin widened, Oksana pierced his midsection from behind with the tanto. It entered just below his rib cage, the blade parallel to the ground. It was all the way in, to the hilt, with the blade's edge facing out to the side. The grin disappeared, replaced by a look of disbelief. Masato looked down at the tip of the blade protruding from his belly. A small amount of blood escaped from his mouth, his eyes unfocused as he looked at Kyle and Aiko. Turning around, with the Guardian still poised to strike and his arms frozen above his head, Masato faced Oksana. There he saw something missing in her eyes, fear.

In disbelief, Masato finally understood that everything in his world had just come crashing down. He screamed. As the Guardian dropped from his hands, Aiko caught it by the handle before it hit the ground.

Oksana stepped away from the display stand as Masato put out his hands to catch his balance on the side of the desk. Not only was he in shock because of his fatal injury, but also because the tanto had been at his disposal since the day he acquired the Guardian and the stand on which it was displayed. Masato couldn't take his eyes off the open drawer of the display stand. The thought kept repeating in his mind over and over, "The tanto, I had it in my possession . . . all this time." For Masato, the nightmare did not end there.

Lining the bottom of the inside of the drawer was an aged leathery parchment inked with a tattoo. He knew what it was right away.

Kyle and Aiko were now standing behind Masato.

Despite his labored breathing, Masato managed to say in a raised voice, "You knew!"

"Enough," Kyle thought, and grabbed the tanto by the handle. Without hesitation, he withdrew it from Masato's body. The wrenching pain made Masato spin around to face his daughter one last time. He reached out and grabbed Aiko by the shoulders for balance. Just before his body collapsed, his final words to her were, "So, the rest of the legend is true. . . AIKO."

Chapter 32

The world seemed especially quiet to Kyle, Aiko and Oksana as they exited Red Sun Exports. Aiko had recovered the scabbards for the swords. She had the tanto in one hand and the Guardian in the other. Oksana had taken Kyle's hand as she walked beside him. Despite the tremendous pain radiating throughout their bodies, they felt good.

"That's far enough," Bogdanoff commanded.

The three stopped in their tracks, fear refueling in their systems. The assassin had a single barrel shotgun pointed at them. Kyle instinctively stepped in front of Aiko who pushed Oksana behind her.

"Toss me the swords, Aiko," Bogdanoff demanded. He raised the shotgun to his shoulder. "I said—"

The killer's words were cut short as a bullet entered his cold, empty heart from behind. His dead body hit the ground the same time his shotgun did.

Pankov lowered his silenced weapon and stood before the trio with confidence in his voice.

"I just saved your life, Kyle. Now I own you, just like I owned your father."

It was then, that Kyle realized it was Pankov who had his hooks in his father, not Masato.

"So, it was you who had my mother killed."

"It was business, Kyle, and your father didn't hold up his end of the bargain."

"What are you talking about?" Kyle stood straighter, ready for another fight.

"Your father tried to play hero one day by attempting to rescue one of my girls from my stable," Pankov paused, giving Kyle an intimidating look. "And that girl turned out to be your mother. Obviously, she wasn't your mother at the time, she was one of my assets. A real profit maker if you know what I mean." Pankov enjoyed the dig into Kyle's family history.

"Unfortunately for your father, he got caught, which left him with a choice. Either he could look away during a few of my special transactions or the girl died. Since your father agreed to my terms, I rewarded him by giving him your mother as a thank you gift."

"My father told me what happened. It's no longer a secret. He's dead, and there is nothing more you have on him."

"I have plenty."

"You're lying."

"Am I? It doesn't matter, because now I own you and your friends. I will offer you the same deal I offered your father. And if you don't agree to my terms, your pretty girls here will have a new outlook on life. First, I will kill you in front of them, then I will kill Aiko, and finally, I will have no other choice but to put the girl back on the market."

Pankov pointed the gun at Kyle's chest.

"What's it going to be, Kyle?"

Kyle turned to Aiko and reached his hand out for the tanto. She handed it to him, an understanding passed between them, reflected in their eyes. Kyle turned back to Pankov and gave him the sword.

"This is what Masato found to be more valuable to him than his own family. Take it."

Pankov took the tanto and drew the small sword from its scabbard. He noticed it still had Masato's blood on the blade. Pankov nodded approvingly at Kyle.

"Now we're even," Kyle said firmly.

"Okay. You don't come after me and I won't come after the girls."

Sirens in the distance broke the confrontational atmosphere.

Pankov said, "You don't have much time."

Kyle nodded in agreement.

"I took the liberty of calling the police as a concerned citizen. I hope you don't mind." Pankov smiled at the trio. "See, I'm not such a bad guy after all."

Pankov turned and walked to a black sedan that had just pulled up to the curb. He got in it and it drove away just before two police cars arrived on the scene.

In the back of the sedan, Pankov had two briefcases. He opened one and took out two swabs used for taking blood samples. Taking the tanto from its scabbard, he wiped the swabs over the blood stains that remained on the blade. When he was done, he put one sample back in the briefcase and kept one for himself. Opening the second briefcase, he removed a large diplomatic pouch. In the pouch, he put the tanto and the blood sample, and sealed it. On the side of the pouch was the seal of the Japanese Embassy.

Kyle was holding Aiko in his arms and Oksana was at his side. "They have your family's tanto and who knows where it will end up."

Aiko nodded to Oksana. "We might have an idea."

Oksana reached into her pocket, pulled out the flash drive, and handed it to Kyle.

Police officer, Skip Baker approached the small group and noticed immediately the unhealthy appearance of all three of them. "Are you alright?"

"Take care of them first," Kyle said as he nodded toward Aiko and Oksana.

"Looks like you need immediate care yourself, sir. What happened to you?"

"It's a long story," replied Kyle.

"I'll call for an ambulance."

"You're going to need more than one," said Kyle.

By now, Baker had been joined by the other law enforcement officers on the scene.

Kyle pointed to the building they had just come out of. "There are girls inside that building that are going to need your assistance." He gave Officer Baker a set of keys and an electronic pass card. "You're going to need these."

*****

The elevator doors opened on the top floor. Officer Baker exited first, joined by his partner, Officer Constantine. They used the swipe key to gain access to the main door of the dorms. The first thing they saw was a small, but unoccupied security station. The monitors showed a guard on top of one of the girls in her room. The guard was quickly arrested and the rest of the floor searched.

In one corner of the floor was a mock casino including a blackjack table, a craps table, and pai gow. Constantine's presumption was that the young girls were taught to be highly skilled at the games. This would have been a huge attraction to the men they were escorting.

In the other corner was a self-sustaining kitchen and dining area for meals. Baker went to the security station and hit the button marked 'Doors.' A series of electronic locks released the doors to the rest of the individual dorm rooms. Girls exited from all the rooms, except one.

Baker entered that room, gun drawn, not sure what to expect. The room was empty, the closet door slightly ajar. Cautiously he pushed it farther open. Hanging from the closet rod was a young girl who used bed sheets to form a noose to end her life. He checked for a pulse, nothing. Her body was lukewarm, an indication they were only minutes too late for this one. His partner passed by the open door with the guard in handcuffs.

"What did ya find, Skip?"

"A real heartbreaker."

The officer didn't know her, only stories like hers. An independent girl from Kentucky, just looking for a job and a place in this world.

One day she's alive, the next day she's being identified by a family member who recognized the small broken heart tattoo on the top of her left breast.

EMTs attended to Kyle, Aiko and Oksana from an ambulance parked by the bay doors at the front entrance. A coroner's van had arrived and as the two attendants rolled a gurney past Kyle, he asked them to stop. He unzipped the black bag to say goodbye to his father. Carefully he removed his father's name tag with the black inlaid letters embossed on the brass. As he slipped the name tag in his pocket, he thanked the attendants for stopping. A wide range of emotions he couldn't pinpoint overwhelmed him as he watched his father being loaded into the coroner's van.

The bay doors behind Kyle rattled as they powered up and he turned to see the six girls he thought were on the third level, walk out. EMTs and officers were already on their way to meet them. Within minutes, Kyle, Aiko and Oksana counted at least twenty-five more girls and some young boys as they continued to file out the open doorway, their hands shielding their eyes in response to not having seen daylight for quite some time.

Aiko silently wept knowing how they felt, that freedom was now firmly in their grasp. She walked to Kyle's side. He put his one good arm around her, their heads tilted so they would touch. Oksana went to Kyle's other side, slipping her hand into his.

The warmth of the morning sun couldn't compare to the feelings he was experiencing as he looked into Aiko's eyes. Kyle didn't know his affection toward her matched the meaning of her name. Beloved.

Made in the USA
Columbia, SC
20 July 2021